Seared
ON MY
SOUL
COLE GIBSEN

Entangled Publishing, LLC
2614 South Timberline Road
Suite 109
Fort Collins, CO 80525
Visit our website at www.entangledpublishing.com.

Embrace is an imprint of Entangled Publishing, LLC.

Edited by Liz Pelletier
Cover design by Louisa Maggio
Cover art from Hot Damn Stock and Shutterstock

Manufactured in the United States of America

First Edition June 2016

embrace

This one is dedicated to my agent, advisor, and friend.
Nicole, thank you for taking a chance on me.

Chapter One

EMILY

The bass beat thumps so loud, pulsing through the ground into the soles of my feet. Several times my heel catches the edge of a pothole, nearly sending me sprawling onto the crumbling parking lot. The triple shot iced mocha in my hand sloshes loudly with each near-fall.

The dumpster nestled against the bar is so full the lid rests halfway open on top of a mound of garbage bags and cardboard boxes. The sickly sweet smell of rot and fried food permeates the parking lot.

Graffiti decorates the entire south wall of the crumbling brick building. A dented and rusted rain gutter hangs on for dear life, held in place by a single screw. The place is a hell pit. A beautiful, glorious hell pit where they serve magical beverages that make me forget all about my sucky-ass job serving lattes and scones to ungrateful hipsters and jackasses in suits — at least for the night, anyway.

I place my hand against the sticky glass door and pause,

casting one last glance over my shoulder. I know he won't be there—and he's not. Habit, I guess. After our dad died, my older brother felt it was his duty to trail me like a shadow. Now that he's in a serious relationship, I guess he has better things to do than follow me around on weekends to make sure I stay out of trouble.

Thank fucking God.

Confirming the lot behind me is indeed free of stalker-brothers, I smile. Despite feeling like I've waited forever for the day I could go out without my brother breathing down my neck, now that it's here I pictured something...*more*. In my head I imagined fireworks and a parade. I saw myself riding in the back of a convertible, waving to my adoring fans, and wearing a sash that read *Emily is a motherfucking adult now*.

The reality is...anticlimactic.

Without Lane trailing me and dictating my every move, I can finally get myself into some good, old-fashioned trouble. The problem is, there's not a lot of trouble to be had in a dull-ass Midwestern town like Springfield, Illinois.

And that sucks.

The front doors of the bar are coated in a yellow haze of nicotine residue. Even though cigarettes are no longer permitted indoors, the smells of smoke, grease from the kitchen, and beer saturate the air inside, oozing into my pores. I shiver happily.

Beyond the crammed dance floor, band members scramble to lug their amps and instruments out onto the stage. Careful not to jostle the drink in my hand, I slide through the mass of bodies, until I reach the smooth lacquer of the bar's edge. I set the coffee down on the sticky surface, only to have it immediately snatched.

"You are a life saver," Ren the bartender shouts over the buzz of voices laughing and shouting. "Triple shot?"

"What am I? New?" I scan the crowd for my best friend

Ashlyn, who happens to be Lane's girlfriend. I introduced them when I took Ash to my brother's studio to get a tattoo covered up. I had no idea at the time Ash was living out of her car to escape her abusive step-dad. Lane rented her the shitty apartment above his studio and it didn't take long for sparks to fly.

I'm happy for them, but I still don't get it. Who knew some girls find "perpetually grumpy" a turn on?

Ren smiles and cups the drink in her hands. She's wearing a tank top and, like me, ink decorates both her arms from shoulders to wrists. It doesn't matter her black hair is pulled into a messy bun or that her eye liner is smudged around her slanted eyes, she looks gorgeous as usual. Lucky for me she's picky with her men—*and* women depending on her mood—so we've never been at odds over a guy.

Ren takes a long sip, after which she sighs. "You're an angel, Em. There was no way I was going to get through the night without this." After another sip, she reaches into the cooler and grabs a cider, twisting the cap off before placing it in front of me. She leans across the bar and juts her chin toward the crowd gathering around the stage. "So, who's it going to be?"

"Not tonight, Renny. It's girls' night. No boys allowed."

Ren leans back, nodding approvingly. "Ashlyn coming up?"

I nod, taking a swig of my drink. A bit of cider dribbles from the corner of my mouth. I lick it, careful not to dislodge the rhinestone piercing above my lip. Along with my rockabilly style, the piercing is homage to my idol, Marilyn Monroe.

"Good," she says. "I haven't seen much of her lately."

That makes two of us, I think, pulling out a tube of red lipstick—the same color as the bandana tied around my platinum curls—and touch up my lips. When I'm finished, I take another drink to swallow the sour resentment burning up the back of my throat. I get that Ashlyn's pursuing her dreams, and I'm super happy she's all in love or whatever—

especially when she makes my brother and niece equally happy. But now that she's either in school, studying, or doing whatever it is in-love people do together, there's very little time left for her to hang out with me.

"Em! Hey, Em."

I glance up and find Ashlyn squeezing through the crowd to get to me. She's not exactly dressed for a night out. Her face is makeup-free, eyes dark and tired looking. Her brown hair hangs slightly askew in a limp ponytail. And she's wearing a paint-splattered t-shirt and a pair of yoga pants. Ashlyn, God love her, has always had minimal fashion sense, but this is a little basic even for her.

I frown. "Honey, you didn't suffer a stroke, did you?" I ask when she reaches the bar. "I mean, you do realize what you're wearing, right?"

She playfully swats my shoulder. "I missed you, too."

Ren deposits a whiskey neat in front of her before spinning away to answer the calls for beer at the opposite end of the bar.

"Thanks, Ren!" Ash calls after her before taking a sip.

"So the outfit…" I prompt. "Did you change plans without telling me? Are we going to Pilates or something?"

Ash rolls her eyes. "You seriously have no idea the kind of day I've had."

"You're right," I agree. "Because I never *see* you anymore."

She flinches and sets her drink back on the bar. "Oh, Em. I know. I'm so sorry. It's just with school, and finals, and—"

She looks so uncomfortable I actually feel guilty for bringing it up. "It's okay. You've got a lot going on. I understand." And I do. Still, there's this selfish part of me that misses hanging out with my best friend. And maybe, just maybe, if I'm completely honest with myself, there's another part of me—a much, *much,* smaller part—that is even a tiny bit jealous. Ash has her life all figured out, while I'm still whipping up non-fat soy lattes for douchebag assholes all day.

I take another long swig from my bottle. I just have to keep that small part of myself drowned in an ocean of booze.

"Thanks." She reaches out and squeezes my arm. That's when I notice the fresh ink on her forearm.

"New tat?"

She glances at her arm and smiles. "Yeah." She traces her finger around the image of a compass with its arrow pointing north. "Lane did it. He has a matching one. Since neither one of us believes in tattooing names, we decided to get compasses. So we can always find our way back home to each other."

I take another gulp of my cider to distract myself from the urge to vomit across the bar. "That's, um, really nice."

She has this dumb, lopsided grin on her face. "Your brother can be really sweet, you know?"

No, I don't. The Lane I grew up with was overprotective, controlling, and had a large stick permanently wedged up his ass. Obviously the Lane she's dating is an alien imposter. But, as long as he continues to stay out of my life, the body-snatcher version of my brother can stay. "New rule," I say, salting a coaster so my bottle won't stick, "no more guy talk during girls' night."

"Oh." She ducks her head. "You're absolutely right. I'm sorry, I—"

I wave a hand in the air, cutting her off. "Forget it. How about we talk about your outfit instead? Because, seriously. You're wearing sweatpants in a bar."

"Yoga pants," she argues.

"There's a difference?"

"*Yeah*. Yoga pants are more refined. They're the classy sweatpants."

I can't help it. I laugh. Which is strange because, even as the giggle bubbles up my throat, sadness squeezes my chest. I miss Ash. I miss the jokes. I miss venting about asshole customers with her. Ever since she quit working at the coffeehouse, we no longer have nights spent talking and stuffing our face with stale cake pops when we should be closing the shop.

Ash laughs, too, and together we giggle until we're red in the face and heaving for breath. She takes another sip of her whiskey between gasps. "I'm sorry I was late. I was up all last night studying, and then I had to pick Harper up from school early because she's sick, so I spent the entire day taking care of her. Lane would have done it, but he's overbooked this week. That's why I didn't have time to change."

My breath catches. "Is Harper okay?"

She sighs. "Lane thinks it's strep. He was getting her ready to go to Urgent Care right before I left."

A thread of worry weaves through my ribs. I hate thinking about my seriously adorable niece suffering. "Because of your selfless act of taking care of my Harper, the fashion police hereby dismiss all charges against you."

She grins. "Well, thank God. I wasn't sure how I was going to afford an attorney." Her phone buzzes with a text. She picks it up. Her brow furrows as she reads. "Oh no."

I set my bottle down. "What's wrong?"

She chews on her bottom lip before answering. "It's Harper. It turns out Lane was right. She has strep. He took her home and asked if I could pick up her antibiotics from the pharmacy."

"You have to go." I fight to keep my disappointment from showing on my face. Part of being a motherfucking adult is understanding sick kids always take precedence over girls' night. So I do my best to ignore the jealousy ripping through my gut, as well as the urge to cry, *That's not fair!*

"Promise me you'll give Harper an extra kiss from Aunt Em?" I ask.

"I promise." Ash hurriedly tucks her phone into her purse and slides off the barstool. "I'm so sorry. I was really looking forward to finally hanging out."

Me, too. Instead of saying so, I wave a hand dismissively. "I get it. I totally understand. We'll just have to try again some other time."

"Yes," she says, inching backward through the crowd. "Really soon."

"Really soon," I repeat, but I don't think she can hear me. Her back's already turned and she's halfway to the door. With a sigh I turn back to my drink and pick at the label. What a sucky turn of events.

Ren wanders over to me with a frown. "Where'd Ash go?"

"Harper's sick," I say, ripping off ribbons of soggy label.

Ren reaches for Ash's whiskey, but I swat her fingers away. "Leave it."

Ren scowls, placing a hand on her hip. "Don't be like that. You still have me. And a whole bar full of potential."

I look up. She has a point. There's no sense in letting the entire night go to waste. After all, the only thing waiting for me at home is half a bottle of flat wine and a DVR full of reality television.

God, why does my life sound so pathetic?

I shake my head to clear my thoughts as I swivel my stool around to survey the crowd. "All right, then. Let's assess our options, shall we?" Even though Ren's bar, The Wishing Well, is nothing but a hole in the wall, she hosts some of the country's best indie bands. This means the crowd is an eclectic mix of college hipsters, rockers, dropouts, music lovers, and the usual drunks. I have options.

I nod toward a muscular guy sitting on a stool in the corner of the room. "He has possibilities."

"Nope." Ren shakes her head. "Girlfriend." No sooner does she say the word when a thin brunette in a barely-there skirt perches herself on his lap.

"Meh." I wave my hand. "There's more where he came from."

"What about him? He's hot." Ren points her finger to a clean-shaven blond guy bent over a pool table.

I consider him for a moment. Sure, he's got a nice ass, but there's not an inch of ink or a piercing on him. In other words, boring. "I don't do J.Crew models." I wrinkle my nose. "I swear, Ren. It's like you don't know me at all."

She snorts. "Oh, I know you plenty, honey. You always go for the biggest player in the place. It wouldn't hurt to mix it up for once."

I narrow my eyes. "I totally resent that. I don't go for the biggest player in the place...I *am* the biggest player in the place."

Ren laughs. "That's my girl." A guy shouts at her from down the bar. She groans and wipes her hands on her apron. "Listen, the natives are getting restless, but I'll be back. In the meantime, I believe what you're looking for is right there." She points to the back of the room.

I follow her finger to a lean guy in a tank top carrying a bass drum onto the stage. Tattoos decorate both of his arms and line his chest. His hair is cropped short on the sides and his ears are pierced with thick black plugs. "A drummer!" I can barely contain the squeal in my voice as I clasp my hands together. "It's not even my birthday!"

Ren rolls her eyes as she slides away. "Do I know you or do I know you? Still, you might want to try something new. Give J.Crew a chance."

I make a face and wave her suggestion away. "I like what I like."

She arches an eyebrow. "Yeah? And what is it about these men you find so appealing? Their loose morals?"

"Close. My ideal man must have the uncanny ability to disappear in the morning." I snap my fingers to illustrate my point.

Ren hands a guy a shot glass of tequila and wipes her

fingers off on the towel tucked into her apron. "I don't know, babe. Sometimes it's nice when they stick around."

I snort and turn my attention back to the man-candy on stage. "I spent my entire life under the watchful gaze of my older brother. Now that I'm finally free, the last thing I want is another man tying me down. At least not before I—" I can't finish the sentence, because I'm not sure how. Before I visit the castles in Scotland again? Drink at the taverns in Ireland for the third time? Skydive for the fifth time? Get a real job? Before I figure out what it is I want to do with my life?

And now that I'm thinking about it, what *do* I want? "I'm still young," I answer myself out loud. "The point is this little birdie is going to stretch her wings before she gets thrown back into a cage."

Grinning, Ren grabs two shot glasses off the rack and fills them with Fireball. Taking a glass in her hand, she slides the other to me. "To freedom."

I pick the glass up and clink it against hers. "To freedom."

Ren goes back to taking orders, and I settle into my seat. The whiskey warms the pit of my stomach and fills my head with a delicious haze. I lean against the bar as the day's tension slowly unwinds from my shoulders. Work was a bitch today. It was bad enough the people wanting lattes was never ending, but top that with a fifteen-minute lecture from some granola mom on the poisonous properties of cow's milk and it was truly the day from hell.

I glance at the drummer bent over his kit as he adjusts the mic stand in front of the bass drum. His jeans are so tight very little is left to the imagination. Maybe he can feel the heat of my gaze searing into his backside, or maybe fate is finally on my side. Either way, he looks behind him and meets my eyes.

He winks.

I can't help but smile as I trace the sticky rim of the shot glass. At least now things are looking up.

Chapter Two

The words on the page blur to inky pools, and I know I just don't have it in me to read one more essay on the Industrial Revolution and its effects on modern commerce. I squeeze my eyes shut and rub my hands down my face.

"Rough night?"

Startled, I jerk back, blinking my eyes to find Tonya, an eleventh grade geometry teacher, standing in the doorway of my classroom. I always thought she was cute, but today she crossed the line into sexy, with her pencil skirt, black-rimmed glasses, and hair pulled back in a bun. For the millionth time I consider asking her out. She's exactly my type—nice, pretty, educated. My parents would love her.

Maybe that's what stops me from asking.

Or maybe it's the bullet hanging from the chain around my neck.

Either way, the words knot inside my throat until I have no choice but to swallow them down. "Yeah." I lean back in my chair and pinch the bridge of my nose. "Industrial Revolution essays. Twenty of them."

"Oof." Her face scrunches in a sympathetic pout—it's adorable. "That'll do it."

I nod, gathering the papers in a stack then stuffing them into my leather messenger bag. "I wanted to be done by now—looks like I'm going to have to DVR the game."

She leans her head against the doorframe. "Cards versus Cubs?"

I zip my bag shut and look at her. "You're a baseball fan?"

She grins. "Don't tell on me, but I'm a Cardinals fan. Big time."

"Really?" In Springfield, Illinois, where allegiances typically run toward all things Chicago, declaring yourself a Cardinal's fan was almost an act of treason. "Me, too."

"I know." Before I can ask how, she says, "I was going to ask if you wanted to grab a beer and catch the game…" Her words lilt with an edge of hopefulness.

Christ, how long has it been since I had a beer with an honest to God woman? It was before I became a teacher. Before the bullet. Before my leg.

I can't help but glance at the cane propped against my desk. All those "befores" added together equal another lifetime—one I can barely remember.

Tonya follows my gaze to the polished wooden staff—a gift from the parents of a soldier who didn't make it home—a gift I don't deserve. "Cane today, huh?"

As if summoned by her words, the pain in my thigh pulses fire-hot. I try not to wince as I rub the ache through my pants leg. "Yeah. Some days are worse than others."

She opens her mouth to say something but apparently thinks better of it before closing her jaw with a snap. I want her to go because she reminds me of everything I once had and can't anymore. I want her to stay because she makes me feel a fraction human again.

I stand, wobbling a bit on my bad leg before settling on my good leg. Tonya moves like she might try and help, and I shoot her a look that freezes her in her tracks. To prove my point, I tuck the cane under my arm, even though pain jolts up my left thigh. I can walk without it, just slower. And honestly? I don't mind the pain.

I deserve it.

Tonya raises an eyebrow. "So, that beer?"

I stop in front of her. She smells so foreign and feminine, like a rose garden. A far cry from the hot sand and diesel fumes that haunt my dreams. I almost relent, almost choose the garden over the phantom stench of decay always following me. But then I move and the bullet sways against my chest. Though the metal is cool, it feels as if it might sear its way through my skin all the way to my heart—where it was meant to be all along.

"Sorry." I pat the messenger bag at my hip. "Papers."

"Right. Industrial Revolution." Her smile tightens. "Rain check?"

"Rain check."

Even though she's smiling, the disappointment is evident in her eyes. *Way to fucking go, Reece,* I scold myself. Not that I should have expected to do otherwise. All I seem to be able to do these days is disappoint people.

She points a finger at me. "Okay, Mr. Montgomery, I'm going to hold you to that."

"I hope you do," I say, and mean it.

Her smile softens. She turns on her heels and sashays down the hall. As I watch her hips rock from side to side, I say a prayer I can find the strength to say yes. A woman would be good for me—the problem is I need a woman strong enough to withstand the darkness I live in. A woman who won't question the ghosts I talk to. A woman who won't flinch when the scent of blood filling my nostrils is strong enough to make me fall to my knees and heave.

In other words, a woman who doesn't exist.

I readjust the bag's shoulder strap and force my hobbled steps into awkward strides as I head out into the parking lot where my motorcycle waits, gleaming like a scorpion under a streetlight. With summer just around the corner, the nights are growing warmer and the humidity thicker. Beads of sweat prick along my shirt collar as I cross the empty lot.

Sheila, my 2010 Victory Vegas 8-Ball, is every bit as sexy and sleek as her name. Before my military tour, I never had an interest in bikes, let alone pictured myself owning one. Chad, however, talked nonstop about buying one once he made it home. That's the funny thing about dreams, sometimes they live on even when we don't.

I unbuckle one of the leather saddlebags and shove my messenger bag inside. Next, I strap my cane to the bag with a pair of bungee cords. I'm in the middle of fishing the keys out of my pocket when the shot rings out.

Despite my injured leg, I'm flat on the ground, tucked behind my bike in seconds. My training is so ingrained, it's practically instinct. But knowing what to do doesn't stop the dread from squeezing my chest like a vise. I've played this game before, only to lose. So why is it happening again? Why here? Why now?

A memory smashes into me with enough force I can't escape it even with my eyes open. I risk a glance around the bike's saddle. The parking lot asphalt is gone, replaced by the rocky terrain of Afghanistan. The distant echo of screams carries from beyond a distant hill. *Chad.* My heart jumps inside my throat, threatening to choke me. *This time I won't fail. This time I will save him.*

But when I try to move, pain like fire washes down the left side of my body, paralyzing me. I look to my leg to find the fabric of my pants sticky and dark. There's a bit of twisted metal protruding from my thigh—a piece of the Little Bird. Instantly the tang of blood burns down my nostrils, and I gag.

The screams ring out again. Wound forgotten, I snap my head in their direction. *Not this time, you son of a bitch.* I reach for my gun, but it's not there. Fuck it. I'll kill the bastards with my bare hands if I have to. I try and push myself to my feet, but the pain is too much. It sizzles down my leg, frying nerves and destroying tissue. I collapse back to the ground.

The screaming continues.

I press my palms to my eyes as the agonized sound swirls inside my head. *Fuck. Not again.* I claw my fingers into the hot dirt and pull myself forward, one excruciating inch at a time, dragging my bleeding leg behind me. *This time I'll save him.*

I've only made it a couple of feet when the screams grow silent.

No.

My throat is thick with dust, blood, and smoke. It takes me several swallows before I can form a word. "Chad!" When he doesn't answer, I try again, louder, "*Chad!*"

"Mr. Montgomery?"

The unfamiliar voice forces me to blink. The barren hills dissolve, and I find myself back at the high school, lying on the warm asphalt.

"Mr. Montgomery?" Caesar, one of the school's janitors stares down at me, his brow furrowed with concern. "Are you okay?"

My breathing comes in rapid bursts that stretch tight across my chest. None of this makes sense. "The shot— someone was shooting—"

"Yeah, sorry about that." Caesar sweeps a hand through his dark hair and juts his chin toward the rusted blue pickup truck parked several spots away. "That's my Bess. She's older now and in need of a tune-up. She backfires every so often."

"A backfire." I touch my pants to find no metal and no blood. Cautiously, I push myself to my feet. The phantom pain dulls to a throb. "Right."

"You need some help?" He offers his arm, which I wave away.

"No. I need—" Actually, I have no fucking clue. Nothing works. Counseling, pills, visits from therapy groups with Golden Retrievers—nothing's been able to rid me of the guilt swelling inside me like a storm. "A beer. I need a beer."

Caesar smiles at that. "Don't we all? Too bad I got toilets to clean." He sighs and turns toward the building. He gives me one last glance over his shoulder before he goes. "You take care of yourself, Mr. Montgomery. When my grandfather came back from Vietnam, he wasn't the same. The war was his personal cancer—ate him from the inside out. Whatever you do, don't close yourself off, okay?" He doesn't wait for a response before he turns and walks toward the school.

Which is for the best, as I'm not sure what response I could give. Even though I think he means well, I'm not a fan of getting advice, especially when it comes to my personal business. And while I can appreciate the horror his grandfather endured in Vietnam, the fact of the matter is, I'm not him.

I climb onto my bike but hesitate before putting the key in the ignition. Instead, I close my eyes and let the silence of the night wrap around me, hoping it'll empty my head. Unfortunately, a dark parking lot does nothing to eliminate the tremor of unease fluttering beneath my skin. For that I need a boat, fishing pole, and the sound of soft waves slapping against a dirt shore.

I open my eyes. I can't go fishing tonight, so I need the next best thing—wind, enough to drown out the screaming. I slip my helmet on, turn the key, and rev the throttle loud enough to rattle my teeth. The knots of anxiety wound inside my gut loosen a fraction. I can finally breathe. I might not be able to outrun my demons, but I'll make 'em run like hell to catch me.

I twist the handle and the back tire catches gravel, swerving slightly before surging ahead. I turn onto the road and gun it. Sheila growls beneath me and I urge her on, giving her more gas until the dotted lines of the road blur together and the wind claws my cheeks.

Together we fly.

I know I'll never fly fast enough or far enough to escape the guilt. But at least for a little while, I'm free. It's that time on my bike, when I'm just a man, with no injuries, no ghosts, and no blood on my hands. Even on my worst days, it's enough to get me through to the next.

It's then I can almost feel what it was like once, when I wasn't a soldier. On my bike, I can almost remember a time when I ventured out of my house for baseball games, and did my grocery shopping before midnight because I wasn't afraid of crowds.

I can almost remember what it was like before I was sent to that sand-covered hell on earth.

I can almost remember when I still felt human.

Chapter Three

My drummer throws a stick into the crowd and I watch, amused, as several girls claw over each other to claim it. Poor things, they have no idea their struggle is in vain. The battle is already over. Even though I've drank enough to blur the edges of my vision, I know the prize is mine.

The lead singer mumbles something into the mic. The crowd cheers. A second later, the lights turn on. Several people groan and shield their eyes. Ren screams for last call at the far end of the bar.

I raise my finger.

Ren frowns and gives a quick shake of her head before snatching several empty beer bottles off the bar. "You know I love you, Em. But you're cut off. Friends do not let friends get blackout drunk and you, my dear, are teetering on the edge."

"Bullshit." I rub my eyes, but it's no use. The two Ren's wavering in front of me refuse to melt into one. "I'm not even buzzed." I slide off the stool to prove as much, only to wobble on my heels. I grab the bar top to keep from falling over while the floor rolls beneath my feet like ocean waves. "Okay, maybe I'm a *little* buzzed."

"You know I'm all about having a good time. Buzzed, tipsy, even drunk are all good as long as you have a ride. You, however, crossed the line into blitzville an hour ago." Ren pops the top off a beer and hands it across the bar to a waiting girl. "Sorry, lady, but it's my bar and my rules. I say when you're done, and you *are done.*"

Anger burns hot beneath my skin. God, even with my brother finally off my back, I still can't escape people telling me what I can and cannot do. "I don't have to deal with this shit," I say, the words fumbling off my strangely thick tongue.

Frowning, Ren folds her arms. Before she can argue, I spin away from the counter. My goal is to storm off in outrage, but my gelatin legs threaten to buckle with each step. Luckily, a hand snags my arm to steady me.

"Where you going, gorgeous?" a deliciously silky voice whispers in my ear. "You're not leaving me all alone, are you?"

I blink several times until the drummer I've been making eyes with all night falls into focus. I have to admit, I'm disappointed. Even with my beer-goggles on, it's abundantly clear he's a Monet—hot from a distance but not much to look at up close.

Damn.

Still, I'm not about to give up my hard-won prize to the ravenous dogs casting dirty looks in my direction. Because if one thing on this planet can make me forget about my shitty life better than booze, it's a good tumble with a hot guy—or in this case, a semi-hot sweaty guy. Being a drummer gives him just enough points to make up for his shortcomings.

I turn into his grip so only inches separate our chests. "Leave you?" I tilt my chin and smile. "Sweetie, I was coming to find you."

He grins. "Yeah? Why's that?"

I trace a finger down his muscular arms. His ink is nice, but not as good as mine. "I have a question I've been wanting to ask you all night."

He arches an eyebrow, waiting.

I push up onto my toes so my lips hover over his ear. "Your place or mine?"

He gives a surprised laugh. "I don't even know your name."

"Does it matter?"

He leans back and appraises me, his eyes traveling the length of my body. "No," he says finally, a smile curling his lips. "No, it does not."

"Good. Then we have an understanding." I bunch both straps of his tank top in one hand and pull him toward the door.

Three girls scowl at me from barstools as we approach. "Slut," one of them calls as we pass.

I ignore her because I've never been able to take that particular word as an insult. Do I like sex? Yes. Does that make me a bad person? Hardly. Besides, no one's shouting names at the drummer as he follows me. I think I even saw one of his bandmates give him a thumbs-up. How is that even fair? If a guy likes sex, give him a high five. If a girl does, better order a chastity belt.

If my brother Lane were here, I can only imagine what he'd say. Probably something along the lines of, "Jesus, Em! You don't even know this guy's name!" As if that's a bad thing. When you give someone your name, you give them a piece of you, and I'm not naïve enough to think for one second this guy's interests in me lie further than my body. So why bother with the whole getting-to-know-you thing? I know how this ends—he'll be gone in the morning, leaving me slightly sore and hopefully satisfied. As long as I'm having fun, not hurting myself or others, where's the harm in that?

I'm almost to the door when Ren calls my name. She's got a hand on her hip and her lips pressed into a thin line. "You've had a lot to drink. You sure…" She bites back whatever she was about to say. "I mean, I can call your brother."

"Thanks for the offer, *Mom*." I roll my eyes. "I'm a big girl, Ren. I know how to handle myself."

Her frown deepens. Fuck if I care. She's *supposed* to act like my friend—not like my boring, overprotective, not to mention all of a sudden prude, brother.

I push the door open. My foot catches on the doorframe and I tumble forward until drummer boy grabs me around the waist.

I fall into a fit of giggles as I collide against him. All that drumming must have paid off, because there's nothing but hard lines beneath the thin cotton of his shirt. I brace a hand against his chest and muscles deep inside me tighten in appreciation of the definition beneath my fingers.

The drummer laughs and curves an arm around my waist, hitching me against his side. "Where's your car?"

I tear my eyes away from his perfect chest. "Why?"

"I don't have wheels, babe. The guys and I share a van."

"Oh." Somewhere deep inside my booze-hazed mind, I realize this is a problem. "I can't drive; I've had too much to drink." I mentally congratulate myself for having the aptitude to realize this. I almost feel like texting Lane just to tell him how responsible I am. Tonight I really feel like I've earned my *motherfucking adult* trophy.

He smirks. "I can drive."

I hesitate. Normally I wouldn't let anyone drive my baby—the 2005 MINI Convertible I bought with years of saved babysitting money when I was sixteen. But since he doesn't have a car of his own, I don't really see another way around it.

I reach into my pocket. The second my fingertips graze the edge of my keys a warning flashes through my mind. Didn't I see girls bringing shot glasses up to the stage for the band to tip back? How many has drummer boy had?

I pull the keys from my pocket but hold them in my clenched fist. "Are *you* okay to drive?"

He laughs. "More than you."

I frown. That wasn't exactly an answer. "How many have you had?"

He shrugs. "A couple. I can't drink when I play drums. Fucks my rhythm all up. So relax, babe. I'm good."

He has a point. "Can you hop on one foot and touch your finger to your nose?"

"If I did that, who would keep you upright?"

Another good point. Before I can stop him, he snatches the keys from my hand and hits the button. The MINI's lights flash from across the parking lot. "There we are," he says. Tightening his grip on my waist, he guides me across the broken asphalt, snickering when my heel catches on a crack and I fall against him.

I laugh along with him even as a tremor of unease bubbles up from somewhere deep inside me. It's quickly numbed by the alcohol coursing through my veins before I can think too much of it.

Drummer boy opens the passenger door and I tumble inside. He hops onto the hood and slides across. When he opens the driver's door and climbs in, I feel as if I should be concerned about something—but for the life of me I can't figure out what. After all, what would be worse than going home to an empty apartment? Alone, I have no way to escape the ever-present stream of doubt coursing through my head. It's bad enough when my mother calls to criticize my life choices, or when my brother brings them up over lunch, but it's so much worse when the voice of regret is my own.

A throbbing pressure pulses at my temples. I reach across the car and wind my fingers into drummer boy's shirt to quell it. Only when my fingers graze his skin, does the throbbing subside.

The guy grins at me. "Eager, huh?" He takes my hand and guides it down to his lap where I can feel the swell of him just below his zipper. "Me, too."

I fight the urge to roll my eyes. *Men.* Always so damn proud of their erections—like I'm supposed to be impressed. There are people working to end world hunger and find a cure for cancer, but you got a hard-on so here's your medal or some shit.

Anyway, I should play nice. I give him what I hope is my most appreciative smile because, let's face it, I need him tonight. What else do I have to look forward to? Another day of making triple-shot café Americanos for college students cramming for their next exam, which will bring them closer to their degree and a rewarding job. Meanwhile, I'll *still* be serving them coffee?

This is so much better.

"Do you want to?" Drummer boy nods to his crotch.

It takes me a second to realize he's asking for a blowjob.

I almost laugh out loud. Maybe *this* particular moment isn't that much better. "This car is my baby." I pat the dashboard affectionately. "We will not sully her. Got that? You get us to my apartment and I promise I'll take care of you."

"Okay." He looks disappointed, but fuck if I care. He's still getting sex—really amazing sex—so he'll get over it. "Where do you live?" he asks.

I withdraw my phone and type my address in the GPS. "Here." After affixing my phone to the holder suction-cupped to my windshield, I settle back into my seat.

The drummer nods and shifts the car into reverse. When we pull out onto the road, the world outside the car windows becomes a blur of gray, navy, and black, like a painting of night sky someone poured water over, blending all the colors together.

I close my eyes to keep from getting dizzy. Maybe I did overdo it just a bit.

"Hey!" Drummer boy's hand clamps down on my thigh and my eyes shoot open. "You're not going to pass out, are you?"

I'm not sure if it's the alcohol or the drummer's driving, but it appears we're weaving across the yellow lane dividers.

"Are you even driving in the right lane?" I ask.

He ignores the question. "Do you know how sexy you are? God, the second you walked in tonight, I wanted to rip your clothes off, bend you over the bar, and fuck your brains out."

Ugh. Okay, so I knew I wasn't climbing into the car with Romeo, but holy hell. The more he talks, the more turned off I get. Too bad I don't have any duct tape handy.

We swerve a little too far into the wrong lane and a passing car blares its horn.

"Jesus!" Drummer boy twists the wheel, putting us back into the right lane.

I grab the door handle to keep from being tossed about. Again, a gurgle of unease bubbles in my gut, but the fog inside my head keeps it from reaching my brain. In fact, the sudden nervousness confuses me. My newly acquired D-list rock star is supposed to eliminate my anxiety, not increase it.

Drummer boy takes a hand off the steering wheel and places it on my thigh. My muscles tense beneath his fingers. "Tell me what you want to do to me."

A wave of exhaustion rolls over me. I open my mouth to answer, but the words aren't there. The truth is I'm no longer sure what I want to do with him, or why I'm with him in the first place. I place two fingers against my temple as if I can somehow dig the answers out. But they don't come.

What the hell are you doing with this loser, Em?

What the hell are you doing with your life?

I drop my hand into my lap when I realize the voice whispering through my head, the one that always sounds suspiciously like my mother's, now sounds like mine.

This is a new development. Usually my self-doubt can't penetrate the alcohol-enforced shield I drown myself in. "First thing I'm going to do is get us both a drink," I answer. That should take care of my voice problem. "And then — "

Drummer boy's fingers dance up my leg. He grins, revealing nicotine-stained teeth.

Ew. I wish I realized he smoked before I picked him up. My disgust clouds my thoughts. Now I have no fucking clue what comes after the booze. My entire goal was to bring home a distraction. Only now I realize my distraction isn't distracting enough.

In fact, the more I look at him, the more unattractive he gets. Holy hell. I quickly look away. New plan. As soon as I get home, I'll simply drink enough to make him cute again.

The sound of the road humming beneath the tires echoes inside my head. The effect is soothing, hypnotic even. Gradually, my muscles loosen and relax against the seat. After a few minutes, I can no longer remember what I was worked up about in the first place.

"Hey. Don't go to sleep." Drummer boy's voice cuts into my head like a knife. His fingers curl around my thigh and he jostles me until I open my eyes.

"I was meditating, asshole. Thanks for making me lose my Zen."

He laughs. "Don't you worry about that. I'll help you find your Zen again and again and again."

I don't bother to keep the skeptic look from my face. I can't remember if I'd ever screwed a drummer before, so I'm not sure if they're all this cocky and delusional, or if I just got the pick of the litter. He's not going to make this easy for me if he keeps talking. Is it possible to screw someone into silence? If so, challenge accepted.

He plays with the button on my jeans and I force myself not to flinch. What the hell is wrong with me? This is what I want. Or at least I thought it was until my own damn brain cut in and planted a seed of doubt. Well, I'll be damned if I'm going to let rational thinking ruin my night.

"Want a little preview?" I lean across the console, place my palm between his legs, and rub the denim softly. He's already hard, practically straining against the zipper.

"Oh God, yeah." Letting out a groan, he closes his eyes and lets his head fall against the seat.

I immediately still. "Dude. You're supposed to be watching the road."

He opens his eyes and grunts. "You need to quit worrying. I already told you I was fine to drive."

His words are like a mental kick in the face. Any sort of distraction I was hoping this guy would bring me cannot break through the growing annoyance I feel for him. "You know what? I think I've changed my mind."

Frowning, he looks at me. "What?"

Ahead, something blurry bounds into the road. Is my drunk mind playing tricks on me? I blink several times, but the shape remains.

"Dude." I snap my fingers at the windshield. "Eyes on the road."

He doesn't look away. "Fuck this shit. Are you seriously fucking with me right now?"

The shape in the road grows larger. I can make out antlers and a white tail. Its head turns, headlights reflecting off black eyes. My heart leaps into my throat, choking me. I point over and over.

Drummer boy finally turns his attention back to the road. His mouth opens and I think he might be screaming, but I hear nothing over the sound of squealing tires. The world spins as first my shoulder bursts with pain and then my head. Flashes of white explode before my eyes like fireworks.

I want to call out to the drummer, but it dawns on me, even in this critical moment, I don't know his name. And he doesn't know mine.

We're going to die, side-by-side, bathed in each other's blood as complete and total strangers.

A tree appears in front of the windshield. When did we leave the road? The shriek of twisting metal and shattering glass pierces my ear drums. When we finally stop, the pain is gone—and that terrifies me more than anything. Shouldn't I feel *something?* I do, however, taste blood, thick and hot running down my throat. There's so much. I cough, over and over, but I continue to drown in it.

I want to open my eyes, but they're glued shut by something warm and sticky. My body feels foreign and loose, like I no longer fit inside it. It's much like the times when I was little and I used to put on my mom's dress coat and heels and flop about the house. I try to move, at least I think I do, but I have no fucking idea if I make any progress.

A new smell overpowers the blood in my nostrils. Burning. It takes me a minute to realize it's gasoline. And then I'm suddenly warm. It's a delicious feeling that glides across my skin, blanketing me from the chilly night air. A tiny siren sounds inside my head, warning me that this warm feeling is dangerous, but I'm too tired to care.

The drummer groans. Or maybe *I* groan. It's like I'm falling deeper inside myself and every sound is falling further and further away.

I want my brother.

I want my mom.

I want anyone but the nameless drummer with ugly teeth.

The feeling of warmth begins to slide away as the sounds grow more distant.

One last pulse of fear jolts through me before it fades, leaving me alone in the dark. If this is the afterlife, it's certainly not what I pictured. Where's the light in the tunnel? Where are the pearly gates? Where are the robes and the halos?

More importantly, where's my dad?

There's nothing but an endless abyss of darkness.

And me in the center of it all.

Chapter Four

REECE

I have no idea how long I've been cruising the backroads. When I'm on my bike and riding the wind, time stops. I exist in a place where history papers grade themselves, I don't need a cane, and good men don't die in their twenties.

In other words, it's a much better world than the one I live in.

I glance at my watch and see it's nearly midnight. The G-SHOCK was a present from my folks for graduating high school. They were furious I enlisted in the army, but they're also the kind of people who honor tradition, and tradition in my family calls for a gift to commemorate any life achievement. They'd hoped I'd take it as an insult, receiving a two-hundred-dollar watch while my twin sister got a new Mercedes for getting accepted into Harvard.

Like a Mercedes would ever hold a candle to Sheila. And besides, I actually dig the watch, which would probably piss my parents off if I still spoke to them, and that makes me like the watch even more. It's a beautiful circle of annoyance and reward.

But my parents don't see it that way. It's always bothered them I don't care about *stuff* the way they do. They don't understand why I prefer my five-year-old Levi's jeans over the designer brands, hardcover books over tablets, and fishing trips to the lake over Caribbean getaways.

The upside to not caring about all that crap is that my parents can't control me with money the way they do my sister. *Do what we tell you and you'll get rewarded* doesn't work when I don't give two shits about whatever shiny thing they dangle in front of me — even when it's my future.

The farther I get from the city, the darker and more winding the roads become. I know if I don't head back now I'll barely be able to function, much less impress any knowledge of history to a classroom of bored sixteen-year-olds. Still, the road beckons me onward, singing a melody of rubber whirling over asphalt, just like a Siren. And I follow her twisting paths deeper, like a helpless sailor willingly led into the depths. I can only go where the song leads.

And so, despite the logical part of my brain that screams for me to go to bed, I pass the turn that would take me toward home and keep riding. It's not like I'd be able to sleep tonight, anyway. After what happened in the school parking lot, the nightmares ripple beneath my skin, waiting to bleed out into my dreams.

So I won't go to sleep. Even if I have to guzzle a gallon of coffee and ride all night.

I take another turn. And another. I lose all sense of direction in the dark but find I don't really care. When you're on the run, it's not the destination that matters, but that you keep on moving. It doesn't matter I'll never get far enough to outrun what hunts me. I can't seem to stop trying.

I slow down as I approach an unfamiliar fork in the road.

My boots crunch against gravel as I survey the area. I glance to the left to see if anyone is coming, and instead spot a faint, orange glow in the distance. It's too late for a farmer to be burning brush. Most likely a couple kids decided to start a bonfire. Not my problem. I turn the wheel to the right and creep forward a couple inches only to stop.

"Damn it." I tighten my grip on the handlebars. I can't say what it is exactly that holds me back, makes me give the blaze a second look. Maybe it's the soldier in me that refuses to stay buried in the desert wasteland where I left him to die. *This we'll defend,* the motto tattooed into my brain during so many months of training, echoes inside my head, reminding me of who I am—or at least who I was. There was a time when I didn't spend all my energy running from my demons. I used to believe in something. I used to believe in myself.

Muttering another curse, I angle the wheel to the left. *Just this once, Reece,* I tell myself. I'll play soldier one more time. But only because it's late and if there is a problem, this far out in the side roads, no one would know about it until morning at the earliest. I wasn't so sure about the whole *this we'll defend,* but the very least I can do is dial 911 should the need arise.

I twist the accelerator and turn left. Sheila growls beneath me, begging for gas, whining to be set free. But I hold back, cruising no more than thirty miles per hour. Because the closer I get to the fire, the more I wish I would have turned right.

Giant plumes of thick black smoke waft from the vehicle angled in the ditch.

Son of a bitch.

I pull my bike to the curb several yards away from the blaze and cut the engine. I don't get off the motorcycle, not right away. Instead, I blink several times, making sure the image before me doesn't evaporate like the desert scene earlier this evening.

But the tiny car with the fire beneath its hood is nothing like the helicopter from my nightmares. I hold my breath, every muscle in my body coiled, listening for the sound of artillery or screams.

Instead, I hear a groan.

Or at least I think I do. It's hard to make out anything over the thrum of my pulse thundering inside my head.

"Hello?" I call out. My only consolation is if this is all inside my head, at least there's no one around to see me make a fool of myself.

Another groan. From the sound of it, several feet outside the car.

Holy shit, this is real.

Adrenaline jolts through my veins like an electric current. I swing my leg over the saddle, the pain in my knee barely registering as the need to act drives me forward. "Where are you?"

The groan again. This time closer and to my right.

I hobble toward the ditch, my damn leg refusing to move as fast as I want it to. When I reach the tall grass I spot him. He's on his back, his face a mosaic of blood and split skin. His hand rests on his stomach, and something about the bizarre angle of his elbow lets me know he has a broken arm.

The dude reeks of alcohol, so the cause of this accident is no mystery. He's just lucky the only person he injured is himself. Dumbass.

Trying to assess the situation, I step closer to him. Without knowing the extent of his injuries, I don't dare move him. Luckily he's managed to crawl a safe distance away from the burning car. I don't even crouch beside him for fear my knee will do something stupid and I won't be able to get up again. "Hey. It's okay. You're going to be fine."

The guy lets out choked little half sobs followed by ragged intakes of breath. Tears mix with blood and run crimson lines down his cheeks.

The blood. The sobs. *Jesus H. Christ.* It's like I'm in the middle of a séance to summon my desert demons. My chest constricts, forcing me to inhale sharply. I ball my hands into fists, tighter and tighter, until my muscles scream in pain. I won't give in to the ghosts, not now. "Listen—Guy? You need to calm down. I'll call for help. You're going to be fine."

"But my arm!" he wails. "It hurts so bad."

"It's broken."

"What?" His lip quivers. "Am I going to lose it?" He tries to sit up, winces, and falls back to the ground. "Oh fuck, oh fuck! I'm going to be a one-armed drummer like that guy from Def Leppard. I'm going to have to learn to play drums with my feet!"

My heart fires against my ribs like rounds from an AK-47. "Hang tight. I'm just going to get my phone." *I'm not in the desert.* I mentally recite the words over and over as I turn and walk back to my bike.

"Where are you going? You're not leaving me, are you?" His voice chokes with panic. "I'll die!"

I grunt. "I'm getting my cell phone to call for help. You're not going to die—at least not today. If you keeping drinking and driving, though, your number's going to be up sooner than later."

He's quiet for several seconds. I'm halfway to my bike when I hear him mutter, "This is all that girl's fault."

Ice shoots up my spine and I slowly turn around, certain I've misheard. "What did you say?"

"The girl!" he moans. "I wouldn't be in this mess if she hadn't talked me into coming home with her."

"There's a girl?" I glance back at the car and see flames shooting out from under the hood. I say a silent prayer this dumb fuck is too drunk to know what he's talking about.

"Yeah. She was in the car with me." He pauses. "Hey, man.

Aren't you going to get your phone? My arm really hurts."

The anger coursing through me burns away any lingering pain, and I march back to the asshole faster than I have since my injury. I bend down, grab a fistful of his shirt and pull him off the ground. The orange glow of the fire illuminates his wide eyes. "Where is the girl now?" I spit between clenched teeth, giving him a shake for emphasis.

He winces. "I-I don't know. She was in the car with me."

I throw him back to the ground and he lets out a yelp. "And you didn't think to look for her?"

"I'm hurt!" he whines.

What a worthless sack of skin. It takes everything in me not to kick the shit out of him right here and now. Lucky for him, I've got a girl to look for.

To keep my strength up, I lift at the gym every other day. But after having my kneecap blown to bits by helicopter debris, cardio isn't exactly my strong suit. Still, I force myself into a stiff, half skip half jog. And while adrenaline keeps me from feeling the pain, I have no doubt tomorrow I'm going to pay dearly for the extra exertion.

The closer I get the more the smell of gasoline burns my nostrils and the thick smoke scratches my throat. The front end of the car is angled down into the steep ditch so that one of its back tires doesn't touch the ground. Several inches of metal are folded back from the front end and flames curl around the hood, blistering the red paint black. It looks like the fire is contained to the hood, but I know that won't last long.

I'm vaguely aware of the sour tang of fear on the back of my tongue, but it's not enough to stop me from approaching the passenger door. In the military, we're taught to swallow terror like chunks of broken glass. Don't think. Just swallow. Even as it's ripping down your throat, slicing into your stomach, and leaving a thousand cuts in its wake.

Don't think.

The heat from the hood sears into my skin like pinpricks from a needle. But I don't flinch. Not even knowing the car could explode at any second gives me pause. Once the switch is flipped, fear and pain are merely obstacles between me and my mission.

And my mission is to save Chad.

I pause, my hand stretched toward the passenger door. No. That's not right. Chad is gone. I shake my head as if to rid myself of the ghost of him, but I know I'll never be free. And I don't deserve to be. Especially not if I fail again.

I try the handle, but the jammed door refuses to budge. "Damn it!" I snarl under my breath. I know I have minutes, maybe only seconds, before the flames spread. I pull on the handle again and again, until I feel as if my own arms will be ripped from my body. Finally, with a squeal of protest, the door gives, and I fling it open.

The platinum-haired girl dangles over her seatbelt like a puppet with severed strings. Tattoos and blood cover her visible skin, making it impossible to pinpoint her injuries. Unfortunately, due to the fire, I don't have the option of leaving her for the paramedics.

Working as quickly as my bum knee allows, I push the deflated remains of the airbag off of her, unfasten her seatbelt, and hoist her over my shoulder.

There's no time to check her vitals, so I say a quick prayer that she's breathing as I stumble away from the wreckage. Because maybe, just maybe, there's absolution in saving a life. Maybe by saving her, I can save a piece of myself.

I dismiss the thought as quickly as it comes. I don't deserve forgiveness and I sure as hell don't deserve saving. Every demon haunting me is a demon earned. And if I have to spend my whole life running from them, isn't that a better fate than Chad's?

An explosion sounds behind me, the force of it driving me to my knees. The pain is like a wave of acid, washing over me and eating into my skin. Still, I hold onto the girl. I won't fail her, too.

Another blast thrusts me chest-first to the ground. I try to get up, but after everything I put it through, my knee refuses to cooperate. Something warm trickles down my face and no matter how many times I blink, I can't bring my vision into focus. Still, I reach my hand in front of me, searching the ground until I find a warm, slender arm. A pulse beats faintly beneath my fingers.

A knot of tension unwinds inside my gut. Still alive. Thank God.

The momentary silence is broken by the sound of sobs from several yards away.

"Get your bitch ass up, get to my bike, and grab my cell phone!" I scream. There's little more I can do at this point. Still, I refuse to be worthless. I scoot myself as close to the girl as I can, curling my body against hers, and shielding her with my back from the raging inferno behind us. Tattooed rose petals peek out from the collar of her shirt—*familiar* rose petals. The realization is slow to surface. I know this girl. She's the loud-mouthed barista who makes my morning coffee.

Thanks to my shitty leg, it's all I can do until help arrives. I wrap my arms around her body, silently praying I'm not jostling broken bones or ruptured organs. The girl is sticky with blood. A sense of helplessness washes over me as I cradle her smaller form. I've been here before, left alone with a body and nothing but my prayers to keep it alive.

This time, I hope they're enough.

Chapter Five

EMILY

My world becomes nothing but pain.

Every breath is a mixture of blood, smoke, and gasoline. From far away, I hear sirens and muffled voices that can't quite penetrate the darkness I've fallen into. Blood, tasting of copper, trickles down my throat. A searing ache, like barbed wire, rips into every inch of my body.

Am I dying?

Terror coils around my gut and I flail in the darkness inside my mind, desperate for anything to hold onto, an object to keep me grounded so I won't fall away. My fingers brush against something soft and I grab hold, twisting the fabric into my fist.

It doesn't take me long to realize the fabric is attached to something—or rather someone—because seconds later a pair of muscular arms snake around my shoulders and press me against an equally firm chest.

It doesn't make sense. I haven't been held this way since

Daddy died nearly a decade ago.

"Can you hear me?" The unfamiliar voice sounds distant, echoing inside my head like a cavern.

I try to answer, but my throat is tight and blood coats my tongue. Instead, I hold tighter, pressing my knotted fingers against his chest. His warmth bleeds into my skin, loosening the fear twisted around my ribs just enough for me to breathe— only it comes as a gasp. "I don't want to die." The words are a surprise, but I realize they're the truest words I've ever spoken.

Unconsciousness tugs at me with velvety fingers, pulling me deeper inside myself. I clutch the fabric in my hands, suddenly terrified that if I'm pulled away, I might not be able to find my way back.

The darkness presses against me, smashing me beneath a wall of endless satin. My fingers lose their grip on the man's shirt, and I can feel myself slipping. Fear rises inside my throat, a jagged lump I can barely breathe around. "Don't," I manage to choke. My voice sounds far away—almost as if it were coming from outside my body. Or maybe I'm the one outside my body.

The thought sends an icy wave of terror crashing over me.

"Don't what?" the man asks, sounding farther away than before. Even so, the panic in his voice is unmistakable.

The darkness grows heavier, and I am too weak to fight. Even my fear ebbs under the crushing weight of exhaustion.

It takes all my remaining strength, but I manage to breathe life into the words tangled on my tongue before unconsciousness consumes me.

"Don't let me go."

Before I even open my eyes, I sense a change. Gone is the tang of blood and acrid stench of smoke. Instead, the smell of antiseptic and bleach burn my nostrils and fill my lungs. I cough, and then cry out, as pain ricochets beneath my ribs with enough force to make my eyes fly open.

Even before I can fully take in the room around me, broken images of the previous night flash through my mind like fragments of a nightmare. Bar. Drummer. Deer. Tree. A blinding flash of pain. The sweet copper taste of blood on my tongue. Smoke. And then a body, cradling mine as I clung to his shirt.

Don't let me go.

My own words echo inside my head, marching in beat to the migraine throbbing beneath my right temple. I press my palm against my head to ease the pain but end up knocking the plastic clip off my index finger. A machine in the corner rings out, its alarm piercing through my skull as the line spiking across a small screen runs flat.

Movement from the corner of the room catches my eye, and I turn my head to see my mother jerk upright, her eyes wide. She's wearing a button-down flannel nightgown over a pair of jeans. Her surprise lasts only a moment before she stands. Her eyes narrow and she moves toward my bed in swift strides.

Shit.

I fumble with the remote next to my bed, hoping to call a nurse. Surely Mom won't murder me in front of a witness. But when I press the button, all it does is raise the head of the bed.

Double shit.

It doesn't matter that I'm twenty-one and live on my own. Mom's tight-lipped frown of disapproval still has the ability to make me flinch. My first instinct is to bury myself beneath the thin sheets and hide. But pain blossoms beneath my skin no matter how slight a movement I make, and I realize escape is impossible.

Without a word, Mom refastens the clip to my finger and

the machine quiets. As a retired nurse, she knows her way around a hospital room. I briefly consider pulling out the IV catheter stuck in my arm—anything to keep her distracted. Because Nurse Lauren is infinitely preferable to Mom Lauren in overall pleasantness.

Mom clutches the bedrail, her knuckles turning white. "Can I get you some water?"

I shake my head, which is a huge mistake. The room teeters on its side as a wave of nausea washes over me.

"You should drink some water." Before I can answer, she grabs a plastic pitcher off a nearby tray and fills a cup. Her hands tremble as she pours.

Guilt swells inside me, pushing against my ribs until I think I might scream from the crushing pressure. "Mom?"

She hands me the cup. "How do you feel? Can you tell me what hurts?" Her eyes sweep over my body before she raises two fingers. "How many fingers do you see?"

I swallow, and my parched throat burns. Still, I don't drink the water in my hand. "Mom, stop. I'm okay." Actually, I don't know if that's true. My entire body aches, but I can pinpoint the source of the pain. Still, I have no casts or incisions, so I can only assume that's a good thing.

Mom doesn't look at me. Instead, she turns to the window. Her shoulders tremble. It's not until the sunlight hits her face that I notice the tears welling in her eyes.

Shame churns through my stomach.

"When the hospital called, I was terrified. Did you know the blood alcohol level of the man you were riding with was nearly twice the legal limit?" she says, continuing to stare out the window.

I blink in response. Actually, this *is* news to me. I saw the drummer have a few drinks between sets, but I never would have handed my keys over to him if I knew he was drunk. I certainly didn't remember him *acting* drunk.

Though, admittedly, after that last shot of whiskey, it's hard to remember much of anything.

"How is…" Too late, I remember I never learned the drummer's name. And now I've admitted as much with the words dangling in the air. Normally, I couldn't care less about other people's opinions of my lifestyle. And by the way Mom's frown deepens, I can tell hers isn't favorable. But then again, I can typically walk away from her when she starts in on another one of her lectures. But given the way she tucks the sheets tightly around my waist, it's becoming clear I don't have the option today.

"Alive," Mom answers, still fussing with the sheet. "Despite his stupidity to get behind the wheel while inebriated, or yours to give him the keys. You know, you'd probably be dead if that man hadn't come by to help. Your guardian angel must have really been looking out for you."

I fight the urge to roll my eyes. If guardian angels existed, where the hell was my dad's the night he got shot? At the thought of him, I reflexively bring my hand to my throat, fingers searching for the necklace—a small silver star—he gave me before he died.

It's not there.

Panic swells inside me like a balloon on the verge of bursting. That necklace is the only thing I had left of Daddy. It was a birthday gift because he told me, "You're the brightest star in my sky, Emmy." I must have lost it during the accident.

As if I didn't already feel like a fuckup. I *need* to find that necklace. "When can I go home?" I try and sit up, but the world rolls around me in nauseous waves, forcing me to lie back down.

Mom gives a little laugh. "If I were you, I'd want to stay in this hospital as long as possible. The sooner you get out, the sooner you have to face your brother."

Oh damn. I flinch. The necklace will have to wait. "Lane

knows?"

"Of course he knows, Em." She throws her hands in the air. "Who do you think drove me here because I was too panicked to drive? You're just lucky Ashlyn kept him in the waiting room until he calmed down. I thought he was going to search the entire hospital for that drunk boyfriend of yours, and Lord only knows what Lane would have done if he found him."

I make a face at her use of "boyfriend" but don't bother to correct her.

"God, Em." She sweeps her fingers through her hair. "You're a smart girl. Why on earth would you get in the car with a drunk driver? I already lost your father; I can't lose you, too."

Her words dig the knife of guilt deeper into my heart. "Mom, I—"

"Were you trying to get yourself killed?" Tears finally break free and stream down her cheeks. "Explain it to me, please, Emily. Because I don't understand why you would do something like this."

Heat flushes my cheeks, and I can feel my face crumple. I sure as hell didn't feel like the smart girl she said I was. I silently will myself not to cry, but that doesn't stop tears from pricking the corner of my eyes. I hate being berated like a child. Even worse, though, is knowing I deserve it.

"Mom, I just..." I open my mouth but the words won't come. I realize there's nothing I can say that will undo last night. Still, I muster enough courage to mutter, "I'm sorry."

Mom's lips press into a thin line. She gives a small shake of her head as if she can't quite believe me. I guess I deserve it. Emily the dumbass strikes again. She grabs my hands and grips them painfully tight. "Don't *ever* do this to me again. Promise me."

Before I can answer, a voice interrupts. "You're awake."

Mom releases me and we both turn toward the door. My brother Lane enters the room. His arms are crossed and the muscle in his cheek is doing that twitchy thing it does every time he's pissed.

Just fucking great. Rolling my eyes, I try to sink deeper into my pillow, as if I could somehow smother myself and, in the process, spare me from the lecture sure to follow. "Well, come on." I snap my fingers. "Let's get this over with, then."

His scowl deepens. Ashlyn, who I just noticed standing behind him, peers around his shoulder. Her eyes are wide with worry. "The nurse said we could come back. But if you're not feeling up to it—"

"I don't care if she's feeling up to it," Lane cuts her off. In three long strides he's at my bedside. The anger radiating off him prickles my skin. He places his hands on either side of my face and touches my forehead with his, like we used to do when we were children. "Are you okay?"

His unexpected concern tightens my throat, and it takes me three swallows before I'm able to speak. "I'm fine."

Lane lets out a long, shaky breath and releases me. "Goddamn it, Emily. We were all scared shitless. You've done some pretty irresponsible shit in your life, but you've really outdone yourself this time."

"Lane!" Ashlyn and my mom scold in unison.

"No," he answers back. "I'm not going to baby her and pretend this is okay." He whirls around and jabs a finger toward my face. "This is *not* okay. Do you realize how lucky you are? You may have walked away with a broken rib and a concussion, but you could have died, Em. *Died.*" His voice cracks on the last word, and it's then I notice how glassy his eyes have become. "We love you, Emily, *that's* why we're so pissed. When the hospital called, they didn't give us a lot of details and we thought—we thought—" Sweeping a hand through his hair, he closes his eyes. "When Harper asked why she needed a sitter today, I lied so she wouldn't worry. I mean, fuck. What do you think it would do to her if she lost her favorite aunt?"

"Only aunt," I try to correct, but my throat's squeezed so tight I can barely get the words out.

His eyes narrow into slits. "Don't try to be cute. I'm so pissed right now I could just—" His fingers ball into fists and he makes a low growl deep in his throat. Ashlyn moves to his side and places a hand on his shoulder. Immediately his fingers unclench and his shoulders relax. He looks at her, his lips quirking up in the tiniest smile. "Sorry."

She squeezes his arm before brushing past him. "Don't be too hard on her. This is partly my fault. Maybe if I hadn't had to leave this wouldn't have happened. God, Em, I'm so sorry." She grabs me by the shoulders and squeezes hard. I bite back the cry of pain and lean into her embrace.

"No." Lane place a hand on Ash's shoulder and gently pries us apart. "This is not Ashlyn's fault, or Mom's fault, or *my* fault. You're always reminding me you're twenty-one, Em, and that you're not a child anymore. And you know what? You're absolutely right. You *are* an adult and it's time to start taking some fucking responsibility."

His words burn and I flinch.

"Life isn't one big party," he continues. "You need to get your shit together. Start acting like the adult you claim to be."

I suck on my bottom lip to keep it from quivering. *I will not cry, damn it!* There are a dozen names I want to call my brother, balancing on the tip of my tongue, but I can't muster the strength to let them go. Because, whether I want to admit it or not, I know everything Lane just said is the truth.

I am a colossal fuckup.

Maybe Lane reads the realization on my face, because his shoulders slump and he sighs. "Something's got to give, Em. I don't want to see you in the hospital again or…worse."

"I know," I whisper. The worried looks shared between him, Mom, and Ash are too much, and I turn to look out the window. What I don't know is what to do about it.

Mom touches my shoulder. "I think you need a change, baby. It might be time to start thinking about a career instead of"—she shrugs—"whatever you're doing at the coffee house. My friend, Sheryl, says her husband's office is looking for a new receptionist. I could have her put in a good word for you."

I fight the urge to roll my eyes. I know she means well, but even if I didn't have tattoos down both arms and piercings, being trapped inside an office would be my own personal hell.

"You could take classes at the community college with me," Ashlyn offers. "It would be fun. We could take the same classes and have lunch together."

Yeah. About as fun as shoving forks into my eye sockets. Still, Ash is my best friend, so I do my best to smile. It hurts my entire face. In high school, when the other kids were studying for their SATs and writing their college entrance essays, I was baking with Grandma, sitting in my bedroom, strumming my guitar, and sneaking out of the house to drink beers with the neighborhood boys. Even then I knew college wasn't part of my future—if only I knew what *was*.

"Look who's awake." A red-haired man with a bun, pointed nose, green scrubs, and a stethoscope wrapped around his neck enters the room. "Hi. I'm Jerod, your nurse." His smile is wide and dimpled. There's a Batman sticker on his stethoscope. He's practically bouncing on his toes with energy. I immediately hate him.

"All right, family." He claps his hands. "Visiting time is over. Our patient needs her rest."

On second thought, Jerod is my new favorite person in the world.

Chapter Six

"That should do it." The doctor, a tired-looking woman with wiry black and gray hair, finishes taping a bandage to my back. She slides away from me on her rolling stool and pushes her glasses up the bridge of her nose. "I'll have the nurse send you home with some ointment. Twice a day, okay?"

I nod, even though I know I'll never open the bottle.

"There's a police officer outside, waiting to talk to you about what happened." She cocks an eyebrow. "You feel up to it?"

I roll my eyes. "Who doesn't feel like being interviewed by the police at four in the morning?"

She smiles. "You did a mighty heroic thing tonight. I hope you realize that."

Heroic. The word grates down my skin, itchy and sharp. That's what they said when they pinned the medal to my chest for watching my best friend bleed out on the sand. I threw that medal in the trash the moment I hobbled out of the plane onto American soil.

"You did good, soldier," she says, patting my good knee.

"How did you—"

She cuts me off with a knowing look and grabs my shirt from the nearby chair. "Is there someone I can call to pick you up?"

A lump wedges inside my throat, but I quickly swallow it down. "No." My sister's several states away. And there's no way in hell I'd call my parents for help of any kind. Even the slightest invitation into my life would result in me having to remove them from my ass with a crowbar. "I'll be fine."

The doc has a strange look in her eyes. Sadness? Pity? Whatever it is, it makes me uncomfortable and I quickly snatch my shirt from her outstretched hand. The moment my fingers curl around the fabric, something small and silver falls out of it onto the floor.

"Whoops," Doc says. She scoops up the item and hands it to me. "How pretty."

It's a small silver star pendant on a thin chain. It must belong to the coffee shop girl. I start to hand the necklace back to her, only to find I can't let go. Memories of last night flood through my mind. I remember her small body cradled within my own. The tremor of fear in her voice as she whispered, *Don't let me go.*

Reflexively, my fingers curl around the necklace and I bring it back to my chest.

"Something wrong?" Doc stares at me, with a furrowed brow.

"The girl—how is she?"

The doc stands and sighs. "She'd be dead if it wasn't for you. She has some burns and a head injury, but she'll live. The driver was drunk. The police are going to take him in after we set his arm."

Good. I almost say the word out loud. That's the least

of what he deserves. I stuff the necklace into my pocket and slide my shirt over my head.

Doc winces, watching me. "You need some help? You should really be taking it easy."

"Nope," I answer, tugging the hem to my waist. Pain is such a normal part of my life that I think I would only be bothered by its absence. Grabbing my cane, I slide off the bed.

Doc gives me a pointed look. "You need to wait for the wheelchair."

"Pass."

She shakes her head. "It's hospital policy. Can I trust you to stay put until I send a nurse with the chair and your discharge papers?"

"I'm not going to make any promises."

Her lips quirk in an almost smile. "*Stay,*" she commands, wagging a finger at me before heading for the door.

"Hey, Doc?" I call out before she disappears. I'm not really sure what compels me to stop her—if it's the necklace in my pocket or something more.

She hesitates in the doorway.

"Do you think I can see her?"

She frowns. "I'm not sure that's a good idea at the moment. While her injuries are not critical, she's getting some much needed rest."

"Sure." I almost reach into my pocket to hand her the necklace, but for reasons I don't understand, I hesitate.

Doc eyes me curiously. "Are you sure you're okay?"

I almost laugh. *Not even a little bit.* But I don't tell her that. Instead, I reach into my pocket and touch the chain. Just knowing it's there loosens the knots in my gut. "I'm good."

She nods, gives me a long look, and disappears through the door. Once she's gone, I pull the necklace out of my pocket and stare at the small glittering star. For the life of me, I can't figure out what I'm doing. I should leave the necklace here, or ask a nurse to take it to the girl. But even knowing what I should do—the *sane* option—I still can't bring myself to let go of the damn thing.

Muttering a curse, I jam it back inside my pocket. I don't have a fucking clue what I'm doing.

What I *do* know is last night, the girl begged me to not let her go.

I guess, for now at least, I'll hold on a little longer.

It's nearly five in the morning when I'm done giving my statement, and I'm officially discharged. Both the cops and nursing staff throw around that *hero* word over and over. Each time I shrug it off like the annoyance it is.

I rip off the stupid wristband and toss it onto the wheelchair a yawning orderly is gripping outside the door of my room. "But-but—"

I ignore his stammering and make my way to the hospital's exit. If I leave now, I'll have just enough time to grab my bike, go back to my apartment, and change clothes before the homeroom bell rings. If I really play my cards right, I might even have a few spare minutes to grab a cup of coffee—

No sooner do I have the thought than the image of the coffee shop girl floats through my mind. It's as if the necklace in my pocket gains fifty pounds, weighing down each step until I have to stop all together.

I mutter a curse under my breath. I know why I can't leave.

I have to return the necklace.

The guys in my squad used to make fun of me, nicknaming me Boy Scout because of my rigid moral compass—an annoying personality trait inherited from my grandfather. I can almost see him now, sitting on a cracked leather recliner, smelling of Old Spice and cigars. Behind him, his Korean War medals are mounted on the dusty mantel in front of a framed United States flag. "Montgomery men are proud," he'd told me. "Honorable men. We do the right thing. Not the easy thing."

And I know he's right. With a grunt, I turn on my heel and hobble in the opposite direction. My knee is on fire, making each step agony, but I know I'd feel even worse if I gave up and went home. And I don't dare take a pill for it—that's a black hole I've watched too many good men fall down.

Ahead of me in the hallway, a man in green scrubs studies a clipboard. His red man bun gives off an unnatural sheen, causing me to suspect it's a clip-in. His name tag reads JEROD and there's a Batman sticker on his stethoscope. He glances up at me as I approach. "Hey. You're the guy who saved the drunk driving couple." He nods. "Really solid thing to do, man."

He slaps me on the arm, and I fight to not frown. I've had more physical contact with people today than I have in the last year combined. It's not helping my mood. "Yeah, about that—do you know where I can find the girl?"

His smile fades. "Oh, I don't know." He touches his hair. The bun moves suspiciously to the left before he quickly drops his hand. "She's resting right now."

"I understand. But I have something of hers I'd like to give back."

He grins. He's entirely too cheerful for this early in the morning. "I'd be happy to take it to her."

I consider giving him the necklace, but then I worry it might not make it to her. I'll rest easier seeing it delivered in person. "If it's all the same to you, I'd rather do it myself."

Jason taps his pen against his clipboard. "I'm not really supposed—"

I can see I'm not making any headway, so I decide to

play the one card I hate playing. "Listen, I'm a United States Veteran. Call it a sense of duty, or even honor, but I have to deliver this necklace personally. I'll leave after. You have my word." I fight to keep a straight face. That speech was a little pretentious for even me.

But it works. Just like I knew it would. I can see Man Bun's resolve crumbling as he chews on his lip. "Fine," he says after a long pause. "Third door on the right. Just be quick, okay?"

I nod, patting his shoulder lightly as I walk by. My knee is screaming by the time I reach the open door and step inside.

The lights are off. The only illumination of the sleeping figure comes from the light filtering through the blinds. Even though her cheeks are swollen and her eyes are bruised, the daylight confirms she is who I first suspected—the tattooed barista from the place I grab my morning cup.

Staring at her, I remember how she felt last night, curled against me as I held her back from the fire. Small. Fragile. My fingers twitch, itching to touch her and confirm she's really okay.

That saving her wasn't just a dream.

But no matter how badly I feel a pull toward her, something holds me back. The way my pulse skips and my chest tightens, I suspect its fear. For the life of me, I can't figure out what I should be afraid of.

A shadow bleeds across the floor in front of me, and I freeze as invisible bands squeeze around my chest. This fear I understand perfectly. *I'm not alone.* The pain in my knee is buried under wave after wave of adrenaline. My muscles tighten, and I turn to face the threat. It doesn't matter if the enemy is real or in my head, I won't be caught off guard. Not again.

Standing in the doorway and blocking my exit is a man about my age—and that's where the similarities end. Tattoos decorate both of his arms and peek out from the collar of his

V-neck T-shirt. His dark hair is long enough to curl over his ears, and a light beard covers his face. Despite the dark circles beneath his eyes, his blue eyes narrow, suddenly sharp.

The look is anything but friendly.

"Who the hell are you?" he asks, pushing his shoulders back.

Behind him, a girl peeks around his shoulders. She, too, can't be any more than twenty. She eyes me curiously.

Reflexively, I grip the handle of my cane tighter. "My name is Reece Montgomery." I touch the small silver chain nestled in my pocket. "I have something that belongs to her." I nod my head toward the sleeping girl.

"Why would you have anything that belongs to her? Are you the guy?" He takes a step toward me, cheek muscles clenching as he works his jaw back and forth.

"The guy?" I ask.

"The son of bitch who thought it was a good idea to drive drunk with my sister in the car?"

His accusation catches me off guard, tangling the words in my throat.

He must take my silence as confirmation, because he reaches for me. Luckily, a bum knee hasn't dulled my reflexes. I duck beneath his outstretched fingers. I'm not sure what he intended to do, but I can assume it wasn't friendly. With his arm still over my shoulder, I grab onto his wrist and twist.

He lets out a grunt and stills. From the angle I'm holding his arm, any movement on his part will result in more pain and possible shoulder dislocation. "You could have killed her, you bastard," he snarls through clenched teeth. "My baby sister, my *only* sister might be dead, and it would be all your fault."

"Guys, stop it," the dark-haired girl pleads, arms outstretched. Her wide eyes dart back and forth between us. "You're going to get us kicked out. You think Emily would want that?"

I glance at the girl in the hospital bed, worried for some bizarre reason she's going to be pissed I'm holding her brother. Thankfully, she doesn't stir. "All right, buddy, I'm going to let you go now. Be cool." I release his arm, not because I have trouble holding him, but because his eyes are brimming with tears. He loves his sister, and I can't help but respect that. "I'm not the driver of the car your sister was in. I'm the guy who pulled her out of it."

The dark-haired girl inhales sharply.

The guy's face crumples, and before I realize what's happening, he has an arm around me, crushing me against his body. He makes a choked noise. "Thank you." He mutters the words over and over. "I didn't mean—I'm so sorry."

"It's cool," I answer, prying myself out of his grip. I haven't been held so tightly by another human since I came back from the desert.

To my relief, he frees me. His eyes still brim with tears, but not a single one has fallen. I respect that, too. "What can I do?" he asks. "How can I repay you?"

I shake my head and take another step back. Only when he's at an arm's length do I find I can breathe again.

"You don't owe me a thing. I was only being a decent human being."

"No, man. I can't accept that. You risked your life for my sister. I have to do something." He reaches into his jeans pocket and retrieves a business card. "Here." He thrusts the card at me. "My name's Lane. I own my own tattoo studio. I'm the best around. You ever want some ink, you come to me, okay? On the house."

I take the card and tuck it into my back pocket. Tattoos have never been my thing, but the thought of how my parents would react is enough to make me smile. "Thanks. I'll keep that in mind."

Lane smiles. "Good."

I glance at the sleeping blonde. Her lips are parted and a small line of drool dots her left cheek. For reasons I don't understand, I'm disappointed she's not awake, though I have no idea what I'd say to her if she was.

"I can tell Emily you stopped by," the other girl says, her voice lilting at the end, waiting.

Emily. Pretty.

"My name is Ashlyn." The dark-haired girl continues to watch me expectantly. When I don't answer, she prods, "I'm sorry. What was your name again?"

"Reece," I tell her. "But you don't have to say anything. She probably doesn't even remember me. I just wanted to make sure she was okay." I turn for the door, only to hesitate as I remember the real reason I came here. "I also wanted to return this." I open my fist and hold my hand open, the silver star necklace still safe. "Here."

Lane's eyes widen and Ashlyn gasps. "Dad gave that to her before he died," Lane says.

Ashlyn takes the necklace from me and cradles it in her hands. "You have no idea what this necklace means to her."

"I get it," I say, thinking about the bullet hanging from the chain beneath my shirt, forever resting against my chest — its intended target. If only Chad hadn't gotten in the way. I don't know what I'd ever do if I lost it, my last and only connection to him.

"Do you want to wait with us? Em's on some pretty strong sedatives. But when she wakes up I know she'll want to thank you."

Em. I like that even more. It's cute. I consider Ashlyn's offer for a heartbeat before remembering school starts in a couple of hours. "Sorry, I have to get going." I turn for the door before they can argue.

"Don't be a stranger, man," Lane calls after me. "You saved my sister's life. I owe you."

I wave as I hobble out the door toward the lobby. The bullet thumps against my chest with every step, as if longing for its original target. A cold sweat prickles along the back of my neck and I sweep my hand through my suddenly damp hair. I hope Lane is right. With the guilt of Chad's death forever trailing me like a shadow, I can't be sure of my own intentions anymore. Last night, when I saw the car was on fire, I sped toward it.

I had no idea who I'd find or what I was getting myself into. Was I really concerned with saving a life — or on some level was I looking to end my own?

Chapter Seven

Emily

The fucker's back again. The asshat in the sport coat—the kind with patches on the elbow. Some days he has a cane, others he doesn't. But he always walks with a limp. And he stares a little too long for my liking, even after I hand him his espresso. He used to come in the shop all the time before my accident, and never acted like a creeper before. But ever since I returned to work, his eyes linger a little too long—and it's *really* starting to piss me off.

He sits in the corner, sipping his drink, looking like a typical suit-wearing douchebag. The only difference is most of the yuppie assholes that come in here don't pay me any attention. And that's just the way I like it.

But not this guy. Even though he's holding a book, his eyes keep darting to my face—probably because it's still black and blue from the accident. Sick freak. I'm about to tell him as much when someone shoves a book in front of my face.

"What the—" I jerk back to find Ashlyn standing behind

the counter, eyes brimming with tears even though she's smiling.

"It's here," she says, hugging the book to her chest. "I can't believe the day is finally here."

"Wait." I wipe my hands on my apron. "Is that what I think it is?"

She squeals and nods.

"Gimme, gimme, gimme!" I snatch the book from her and run my finger through the list of names on the cover until I find hers. I can't help but grin. "Oh my God, this is amazing."

"I know. It's so amazing to see my name in print, even if it is just an anthology."

"Just?" I snort and hit her lightly upside her head with her own book. "Don't you dare downplay this. Being published is a huge deal."

Her cheeks burn crimson and she ducks her head.

"This calls for a celebration!" I set the book on the counter and grab a plastic cup. "One iced mocha on the house."

"Yay." Ash claps her hands. "I can't believe I've only been published for a day and I'm already enjoying the perks of being a famous author."

"Get used to it, baby," I reply, pouring milk into the cup. I make sure to use whole milk. Even though Ash has gained weight since her days of being homeless and living out of her car, she could stand a little more meat on her bones. When I'm finished making her drink I slide it across the counter. "And the party doesn't have to stop here. Just because I'm in A.A. now doesn't mean we can't find a fun booze-free way to celebrate."

Ash makes a choking noise mid-sip and sets her drink on the counter. "I'd love that, Em, it's just that, um, Lane made reservations and—"

Of course he did. I turn away, feeling suddenly stupid. *God, I'm an idiot.* I shrug. "No biggie. We can do it another night."

"Don't be silly. It won't be a celebration if you're not there. It would be no trouble at all to change the reservation and—"

There is no way in hell I'm going to play the pathetic third wheel. I turn to face her. "Ash, it's fine. Really." I force a huge smile. "Spend the night celebrating with your man. I'll take a rain check." *Just add it to the pile*, I silently add.

"But—"

I hold up my hand to silence her. I refuse to accept a pity invitation. There's nothing I hate more than people feeling sorry for me—and it's only gotten worse since the accident. I wrack my brain for a way to keep her from looking at me like I'm a limping lost puppy. What would make me less a loser? A Nobel Peace Prize nomination? A Paris photo shoot?

No good. I need something realistic. So naturally I blurt out the first non-ridiculous excuse that came to mind. "You know what? I completely forgot—I can't go out tonight anyway. I…have a date."

Shit. The second Ash's eyes widen I know I've used the wrong excuse.

"What? A date? A real one? Like my kind of date or your kind of date? Do I know the guy? Where did you meet him?" She narrows her eyes. "Are you supposed to be dating while in recovery?"

Yeah. Definitely wrong excuse. I purse my lips. "It's fine, *Mom*. It's just one date. Actually, it's not even a date. Just coffee. And talking. By those standards, what we're doing now would be a date. So no. Definitely not a date."

She frowns. "I don't think Lane—"

"Has to know anything about it," I interrupt. *Shit, this lie is becoming more complicated by the second.*

"Are you sure we can't change the reservation?" Ash asks. "It would be so easy. And a double date would be really fun."

I shake my head as I pick crumbs off the counter. "I don't

think that's a good idea for the first date. I don't want him to feel ambushed, you know?"

"You're acting really weird about this." Ash crosses her arms. "Who is this guy, anyway?"

I grab a discarder straw wrapper, roll it into a ball, and flick it into the trash. "You don't know him."

"Where did you meet?"

"Here at the coffee shop."

"What does he do for a living?"

I make a face. "I don't know his life story, Ash. He only asked me out today."

She gives me a pointed look. "What's his name?"

"Why are you making such a big deal about this?" I snatch a rag and begin to wipe the counter furiously in an attempt to hide my frustration.

"Can't I be interested in my best friend's love life?" she asks.

I stop scrubbing. "You're not going to let this go, are you?"

"Nope." Smiling, Ash shakes her head.

"Fine." I throw the rag on the counter and scan the room. I'll distract her with a random guy, tell her the date was a bust, and that will be the end of that. Unfortunately for me, the only guy in the café remotely close to my age is sport jacket creeper dude. With a sigh, I wipe my hands on my apron. "Wait right here," I tell her.

I march over to the creeper who's still sitting in the corner with his book. He frowns slightly as he watches me approach. He's everything I don't like in a guy—collared shirt, clean-shaven, and not a tattoo to be seen. *Ugh, boring.* Lucky for me, this is all just pretend.

I stop beside him and place a hand on my hip. "I need you to do me a favor."

His frown deepens and he sets his book down. "What?"

I huff. "Trust me, you're the last guy I would ask for this

favor, but you're the only guy in here under fifty. See that girl over there?" I motion toward Ashlyn. Her eyes are so wide I'm sure they're seconds from falling out of her head. "That's my best friend. Do me a favor and pretend we're going on a date tonight so I can get her off my back."

He jerks slightly. "What?"

"Not for real," I tell him. "Just say we have a date tonight and then you and I can go our separate ways and pretend this whole thing never happened. I'll give you free coffee for the rest of the month. What do you say?"

He opens his mouth to answer when Ashlyn appears at my side. "Reece. I can't believe it's you." She holds her hand out. "Ashlyn, remember?"

Reece smiles politely and shakes her hand.

Oh, fuck me. Ash knows this guy? I can practically feel the blood drain from my face.

"I can't believe this," Ash continues. "You and Em are going on a date?"

He turns, giving me a hard stare. I clasp my hands beneath my chin and mouth the words, *Free coffee.*

He grunts. "Apparently." Grabbing his cane, he pushes to his feet. "I hate to leave so abruptly, but I need to get to class before my students do."

Perfect. I smile inwardly. Leave now and everything will be fine.

"Wait." Ash grabs his arms. "Lane and I have reservations at Alfonso's tonight. Em didn't think you'd want to double date because you'd feel awkward, but since you already know us, please say you'll come. Lane would love it."

Lane? My heart plummets to my stomach. This guy knows my brother, too? A siren rings though my head along with the warning: *Abort. Abort. Abort.* I shoot Reece a panicked look.

He shifts awkwardly. "Yeah, I don't think that's such a good—"

"Please," Ash interrupts, tugging on his arm. "Let us take you out—our treat. It's the least we can do after everything you've done."

Reece looks to me, but I'm too stunned by what Ash said to respond. Why the hell do they owe douchebag Sport Coat anything?

"Great," Ashlyn says before either of us can answer. "We'll see you at eight."

We both blink at her. Finally, Reece breaks the silence. "I better get going."

"I'll walk you out," I announce, wrapping my arm around his. He immediately stiffens but allows me to hold on. Once we're through the door, I let go. "What the hell was that? You weren't supposed to agree to an actual date. It was supposed to be fake, remember?"

He glares at me. "I don't remember you stepping in to say anything."

"Oh my God." I run my fingers through my hair. "This is perfect, just *fucking* perfect."

"I don't know what you're so upset about," he says. "You said yourself, it's just pretend. Tell them I cancelled or something."

I groan. "You don't get it. I don't want anyone feeling sorry for me, and if they think I got stood up, they're really going to think I'm pathetic."

He leans on his cane. "So what's your solution?"

"We have to go on the date. Duh."

"Nope." He shakes his head. "I did not agree to that. Actually, I didn't agree to any of this."

"No, but you didn't *not* agree to it, either. It's your fault I'm in this mess. Besides, what else do you have going on tonight? Another hot date?"

He pauses, frown deepening. "No. I don't date."

I feign surprise. "With that award-winning personality?

I'm shocked, I say. *Shocked*."

His scowl deepens. "If you were such a hot commodity yourself, why would you have to beg strangers to take you out?"

Ouch. I fight to keep from flinching. "Listen, I just don't understand what the big deal is. All we have to do is pretend to be mildly interested in each other for approximately an hour. We get to eat good food without doing dishes. And if we play our cards right, we're both in our separate homes, watching our separate Netflix accounts, by ten o'clock."

He's quiet for a moment before finally letting out a long sigh. "This is insane, but whatever. You win. I'll go on your fake date. But just so you know, I'm not picking you up and I'm not paying for your dinner."

"Never asked you to."

"I'll meet you at Alfonso's, I'll stay through the meal, and afterward I'm gone."

"Good."

"Great," he echoes.

We stare at each other for several heartbeats, like children having a staring contest. And me being who I am, even though my eyes are burning, I refuse to blink.

Reece is the first to break the silence. "Don't you have coffee to make or something?"

"Don't you have a class to teach?" I counter.

He mumbles something under his breath and hobbles toward a line of cars. I half expect him to climb into the Volvo sedan, but instead he straddles the sexiest motorcycle I've ever seen.

I hide my obvious surprise with a snort. He's way too straight-laced and boring for a bike like that. Either he's borrowing it from a friend or he's overcompensating for some serious bedroom issues. If it's the latter, lucky for me I'll never have to find out.

The bike's tires squeal as he peels out of the parking lot.

Definitely bedroom issues. I pity the girl who has to deal with *that*.

I walk back toward the coffee house to find Ashlyn waiting for me by the door.

"This is unbelievable," she says as I approach.

"What? That I have a date?" I place a hand on my hip. "Thanks for the optimism."

"No." She hits me lightly on the arm. "That you have a date with *Reece*."

That's right, I remember. "Say, how is it exactly that you know him?"

Ash jerks back, her eyes widening. Instantly, I know I've said the wrong—and probably stupid—thing. "I know him the same way that you do." She pauses, as if waiting for me to draw some conclusion. When I don't react, she clasps her hands over her mouth. "Oh my God." Her words are muffled by her fingers. "You have no idea, do you?"

"Of course I do." I pretend to wipe an invisible stain off a nearby table. "We met here at the coffee shop. He comes in nearly every day." At least that much is true.

"And?" she prompts.

"*And,*" I shrug, "that's it."

"No, it's not." Ash grabs my hands, forcing me to meet her gaze. "Emily, Reece is the guy who saved you the night of the accident. By some miracle, he happened to come across your wreck while he was out riding his motorcycle. He pulled you from your car and later, at the hospital, returned your necklace." She touches the star pendant at the nape of my neck.

"What?" For several dizzying seconds I feel as if the floor beneath my feet has crumbled and left me in a spiraling freefall. "That can't be right."

"It's true. I met him at the hospital when he came to your

room to return your necklace." She places a hand on my arm, and it's her touch that stops my falling, anchoring me to the room, to the moment…to the truth. "Em, Reece saved your life that night."

"Why didn't he say anything?" I mutter.

Ash clasps her hands together. "Maybe he didn't want that to influence your decision to go out with him. Maybe he wants you to like him for who he is and not what he's done for you." She sighs. "Isn't that romantic?"

I give her a little smile. I wouldn't want to shatter her delusion with the much less romantic truth—that I guilted the guy who saved my life into agreeing to a fake date with me so I wouldn't look like a pathetic loser to my best friend and brother.

And worse still, despite the fact I feel like the world's biggest idiot, now I'm going to have to be nice to him—at least for the night.

Chapter Eight

REECE

"Another late night grading papers, huh?" Tonya stands in the doorway to my classroom. She's wearing her hair down today. It spills across her shoulders when she tilts her head. A few tendrils fall into her cleavage.

My mouth goes dry, forcing me to grunt an acknowledgement.

She taps her dimpled chin with a manicured nail. "I've been doing the same thing. What a coincidence." She approaches my desk and I can feel heat flush up my neck. Again I'm reminded how very long it's been since I've been with a woman. To distract myself, I shuffle the papers into neat, meaningless piles.

Tonya perches on the edge of my desk. "Looks like you're all finished."

"Yup." I shove the stacks of half-graded papers into my messenger bag.

"Another coincidence. Me, too." She glances at the clock

on the wall. "Dinner time. I'm starving. You got any plans?" She gives me a hopeful look.

I pause. I know I'd have a much better time with her than I would the tattooed-loudmouth barista. But even at the thought of standing her up—even for a fake date—makes my gut clench with guilt. I really am a Goddamn Boy Scout. "Unfortunately, yes."

Her face falls, making me feel like a royal ass. For reasons I don't understand myself, I've yet to make good on my promise for a rain check. Aside from being sexy as hell, Tonya is an amazing woman. She coaches the JV volleyball team, heads the school's animal activists' club, and is always pestering faculty to volunteer on her Habitat for Humanity projects.

So why can't I bring myself to ask her out? What the hell is wrong with me? Maybe it's all that wholesome goodness she projects. She's so innocent—unblemished by the world I've seen and the darkness it holds—the darkness that now resides within me.

Tonya gives me what appears to be a forced smile. "Unfortunately?"

I exhale. "I got roped into this thing tonight. It's going to suck."

She arches an eyebrow. "Thing?"

I know she's not going to quit until I tell her. "It's a date, but not a real one."

If my admission has any effect on her, she doesn't let it show. "How can a date not be real?"

"When it's done out of guilt," I say, zipping my bag closed. I grab my cane. "Or pity." The only problem is, between Emily and myself, I can't decide who's more pathetic.

"So how you'd get roped into that?"

"That *is* the million dollar question."

"If it's going to be that bad," she says, "just cancel."

I shake my head. "I can't do that."

"Why?"

"Because that would be really shitty of me. I agreed to do this, so the least I can do is see it through. I won't bail out, no matter how badly I want to."

"Or don't want to."

I jerk back. "What?"

Hopping off my desk, she gives me a sad smile. "You're a grownup, Reece. You have the option of not doing something you don't want to. And since I don't see a gun to your head, I have to wonder if there's a small part of you that really wants to do this."

I open my mouth to argue, but she cuts me off. "I hope you have a nice time. You're a great guy and you deserve every chance of happiness." She smiles before walking out of the room.

I stare at the door long after she's gone. There's no way she's right—that I *want* to go on a date with the loud-mouthed barista. Emily's rude, pushy, and obviously a party girl. She's the exact opposite of the type of girl I used to look for before I gave up dating.

So why don't I cancel? Tonya's absolutely right. I'm a grown man. I don't have to do this if I don't want to.

Unless you do want to, Tonya's words echo through my brain.

Ridiculous. I shake my head as if to dislodge the words from my head. I'm the Boy Scout. I agreed to do this out of pity, so I'm going to see my commitment through. There's nothing more to it. I glance at the clock. It's a pity date I'm dangerously late for. When I'm ready to date—*really date*—Tonya will be the first to know. I only hope she won't have given up on me by then.

I swing my messenger bag over my shoulder, lock my classroom, and trudge out to the parking lot. Sheila waits for me, hunkered next to the lamppost, almost as if she knows where I'm going and she's pouting.

"It's a pity date," I say again, patting her gas tank. "You're still the only woman for me." With that, I rev the engine and pull onto the road.

Fifteen minutes later, I pull into Alfonso's parking lot, which is filled almost entirely with German imports. The outside of the brick restaurant is lined with gas lamps and landscaped with large leafy plants. It's the sort of stuffy place my parents were always dragging me and my sister to when we were kids. The kind of place where you had to sit up straight, keep your napkin on your lap, and know which fork to use for the salad and which to use for the entrée.

Pulling my helmet off, I sigh. I hate places like this.

I trudge up the walkway only to stop when I spot Emily.

To my annoyance, my throat, along with another unmentionable muscle, tightens. She looks like she just stepped out of a greasy auto body shop pinup calendar.

I don't move for several seconds, giving myself time to enjoy the view before I'm spotted. She studies her phone, leaning against one of the brick pillars flanking the entryway. She's wearing a black high-waist pencil skirt, a red blouse with short lacy sleeves and the top two buttons undone, and black pumps. Her platinum curls have been rolled and pinned around the red handkerchief tied in her hair.

She looks up, meeting my eyes, and it occurs to me my palms are sweating.

"What are you doing?" she asks.

Giving myself a mental shake, I march toward her. "Knee's bothering me tonight," I lie, hoping not to look more like an idiot than I already do.

She waves a hand dismissively. "You're not going to believe this. They're not coming. Un-fucking-believable."

An older couple walking by stops to gape. Even though

I wasn't the one who cursed, I can feel an apology bubble up my throat—thanks to all the years of being schooled by my parents on manners. Emily, however, glares at them until they move on.

What the hell did I just get myself into?

"Look," she says, raising her phone inches from my face. It's a text from Ashlyn that reads:

Please don't kill me. Your mom caught Harper's strep. And since she was our babysitter, it looks like we're not going to be able to make it. Please have fun without us. The reservation is under Lane's name.

"Can you believe this shit?" she says, tossing her phone into a clutch. "They're standing us up. Looks like you're off the hook."

The relief I expect to feel doesn't come, and that confuses the hell out of me. "Oh. Great."

She bites her lip and looks at her feet. "Look, I'm sorry about roping you into this mess. Sometimes I can be a little, um, impulsive. Just because I was feeling pathetic doesn't mean I should have dragged you into it. I'm, uh, sorry."

Her admission catches me off guard. This girl has a bigger wall than China, and this is the first glimpse I've seen beyond it. "Actually, this wasn't an entirely horrible idea. Real or fake, I haven't been out in"—I swallow—"well, a long time. So in a way, it's a step forward for me. So thank you."

She gives me a smile. An honest to God genuine smile. It all but knocks me off my feet. Maybe I never noticed before because tattoos and piercings aren't my thing, but looking at Emily now, really seeing her, she's absolutely stunning.

"Well, I got to tell you one thing, Reece," she says. "Of all the almost-dates I've had, this has been the best."

"Yeah? Mine, too."

We stare at each silently until her smile fades. "I guess I'm going to call an Uber. You are relieved of duty, soldier."

I flinch at the last word. I think she notices. Squinting, she studies my face, searching for...I don't know exactly. Whatever it is, I look away before she can find it. I glance at my watch. "It is getting late."

"Yeah."

"And I'm starving."

"Me, too."

I know it's a bad idea before the words leave my mouth. And still, I say them. "You know, we're both hungry. It would be stupid if we didn't get something to eat. And how awful would it be if we did it together? Just two people getting a meal and having a conversation. Could be fun. Could be awful. At least it won't be boring."

Her lip twitches in an almost grin before she looks at the door and it dissolves completely. "This kind of place really isn't my scene."

"Mine, either."

She arches an eyebrow. "Bullshit." She nods her chin at me. "Sport coat. Gold watch. Are those loafers?" She laughs before I can answer. "Good God, you look like you were raised in a place like this."

I glance into the window, at the row after row of middle-aged white couples dining in their suits and pearls. "I was," I acknowledge.

"So how can you say this isn't your scene?"

"Let's just say my parents had this mold they wanted me to fit in. And no matter how hard I tried, I never could."

She gives me a thoughtful look before blurting, "I like pizza. And burgers."

"Great." I swivel around on my cane. "I know the perfect pizza joint not far from here." I start for my bike. "I'll drive."

"I know you're the one who pulled me out of my car the night of the accident."

I freeze. I figured Ashlyn would tell her once I left. But

it still bothers me. I like us being on neutral ground, and this feels anything but. "Yeah?"

"You saved my life."

It's not a question, so I don't bother answering. Instead, I walk the rest of the way to my bike and hike my leg over the saddle. "You coming?"

"Just so you know," she continues, "that while I'm thankful, it doesn't mean I *owe* you anything, if you catch my drift."

I jerk back. "First of all, whatever you're *implying*, let me start off by telling you that had never crossed my mind. If I wanted to get laid, I can think of a dozen easier ways to go about it other than pulling women out of burning cars. Secondly, what the hell is wrong with you that you'd even think that?"

"Oh, honey." She brushes past me, trailing her fingers along my chest as she does. "That would take months, maybe even years for you to figure out." She stops beside Sheila, pulls up her skirt, flashing a dangerous amount of leg, and climbs on behind me. "And we've got only one night."

Chapter Nine

EMILY

Had I known I would be clinging to a man on the back of his motorcycle, there's no way in hell I would have worn a skirt. I had to hike the hem up way above my thighs just to straddle the stupid thing. To top it off, I have to cling to this strange man just to keep every other motorist on the road from getting V.I.P access to the Emily Garrett skin show.

Actually, if I'm being honest, I don't mind the clinging *that* much. Despite the warm summer evening, the wind carries a chill that Reece's body wards off. Not to mention he smells amazing, minty with a hint of citrus. And apparently his injury doesn't keep him from the gym. I can feel the ripples of hard muscle beneath the stupid sport coat I'm wrapped around.

Reece pulls into the parking lot of a dimly lit pizzeria and cuts the engine. I'm hit with the aroma of garlic and cheese, and my stomach roars to life. I remove Reece's helmet—his only helmet, that he insisted *I* wear—and go about patting my head for stray hairs. *Not* that I care about what I look like or impressing him.

After hopping off the bike and retrieving his cane, Reece extends his hand. I stare at it for several seconds before I realize he means for me to take it. It's so ridiculous I have to muffle a snicker. Outside of the movies, I wasn't aware men still did that. Still, I'll play along. If he wants to be a gentleman, I guess I can act the part of the lady—at least for the night.

I slip my fingers around his and allow him to help me off the bike. The gesture is so foreign to me, I wrack my brain for the last time a guy helped me into or out of their vehicle.

I come up with nothing.

It's not like I need that sort of treatment. I'm not a helpless princess. It's probably something yuppie guys like Reece learn from their yuppie dads to work stuck-up girls out of their panties. And I'm a strong, independent woman. That shit won't work on me.

But I'd be lying if I said that a teeny-tiny part of me didn't like it.

When my feet are planted firmly on the ground, Reece extends his arm.

I almost laugh. This guy is un-fucking-believable. "I can walk, you know." I motion to the cane. "Probably better than you can."

He frowns and drops his arm as we walk side by side to the restaurant. "I wasn't trying to piss you off," he says. "I thought I was being polite."

"You don't have to do that shit." He reaches in front of me for the door handle, and I snatch it before he can. "Not with me."

He holds his hands up in surrender. "My apologies. I didn't realize I was offending Her Majesty, Queen Badass."

I make a face. "I'm just reminding you, this isn't a real date."

His scowl deepens. "I know."

"Then you're wasting your time on me with all that

chivalry shit. It's not going to get you anywhere."

To my surprise, he laughs. "You think I'm trying to seduce you? Emily, I open doors for everyone. I do it out of respect."

For reasons I don't understand, his admission makes me feel uncomfortable. I try to hide this by placing a hand on my hip. "Why on earth would you respect me?"

He reaches past me and opens the door. "Why wouldn't I?"

Because I'm an alcoholic. Because I'm a barista with no plans for the future. Because guys like you would never in a million years go for a girl like me. These reasons and more flood my brain before I can stop them. I shake my head, trying to loosen them. *God, where the hell is this coming from?* "Never mind," I mumble, walking through the door.

I don't need the voice of my own self-doubt harassing now, especially when I'm trying so hard to give up drinking.

I have to walk sideways through the cluster of people standing around the hostess podium. To my left, three families are squeezed on the lone bench against the wall. Music blares from a jukebox, barely audible over the buzz of conversation.

"Holy crap, it's crowded," I say over my shoulder. "At least we know the food's good." I dodge elbows and squeeze past bodies until I reach the podium.

A bored-looking teenager glances up from her seating chart. "Just one?"

"Uh, no." Does she need glasses? I turn to Reece in the hopes of having him chime in, only to notice he's not with me. *What the—?* Rising to my toes, I peer over the shoulders of crowd around me to spot him by the door. "Reece." When my call doesn't get a response, I shout. "Reece!" Still, nothing.

I hold a finger up to the hostess. "Mark us down for two under the name Emily. I'll be right back." Annoyed, I weave my way back through the crowd. *What the hell happened to his chivalry?* I find him just inside the door. "What's up?" I ask, stopping in front of him. "Did you change your mind?"

He doesn't answer, doesn't move, doesn't blink.

A chill starts at the base of my spine, winding up each vertebra all the way to my neck. "Reece? Are you okay?"

He inhales sharply, blinking, but it's as if his eyes refuse to focus. "I just—" He swallows. "It's been a while since I've eaten out. It's loud, isn't it?"

"Yeah? So?"

He says nothing. His chest shudders as his breathing becomes shallow. His hand flexes on his cane, fingers tightening then relaxing. His knuckles flex to white, to pink, to white again.

"Jesus, Reece." I hold a hand out to touch him, but fear keeps my fingers hovering above his shirt. "What's happening? What's wrong?"

"Hey, buddy." A large man appears in the doorway behind Reece. He's taller than Reece by six inches and nearly twice as wide. "Can you get out of the way?"

Reece doesn't budge.

The guy gives an impatient huff. "Are you deaf?"

"Can't you see something's wrong, jackass?" I ask. "Chill the fuck out and give us a minute."

The man's brow folds like dough. "You can't talk to me like that, bitch. And you sure as hell can't block the door. Now, move."

Reece isn't even looking at him, but the second the big guy's meaty hands reach for his shoulder, it's like Reece gets struck by a bolt of lightning. He jerks upright, standing taller than I thought possible for a guy with a bad leg. Reece clasps the man's wrist and bends it. He swings the guy in front of him and drives him to his knees.

The man squeals in pain, but Reece holds firm.

"Reece! What are you—" Before I can get the words out, I notice his face. His teeth are bared, his eyes feral like an animal's.

My throat tightens and I take a step back. "Reece?" This time, when I speak his name, it's barely a whisper.

He blinks. The change that follows is slow. His lips uncurl, his muscles relax, and finally, his eyes soften. He follows my gaze to the wrist clutched in his hand and the sniveling man it belongs to.

"Shit." Reece lets go and scrambles backward.

The big guy cradles his arm to his chest and scrambles to his feet. "What the hell is wrong with you, man?"

It's then I notice the restaurant has fallen silent. Every pair of eyes is turned in our direction. A man at a far table stands, fists clenched. A young mother pulls her child out of the highchair and onto her lap. The bored hostess actually looks interested.

"I'm sorry." Reece presses a fist against his temple. "I didn't mean—shit."

Part of me wants to go to him, but another part is scared to move any closer.

"What's going on out here?" A balding man in an apron emerges from the swinging kitchen door and pushes his way through the crowd. The name John is embroidered on the black apron in red thread.

"You need to call the police," the big guy says, pointing a finger at Reece, who now stands with his back flat against the wall. "That lunatic over there assaulted me."

Several people murmur their agreement.

"That's a lie." I move, positioning myself between Reece and the gorilla. "This asshat started everything." I don't care if we get kicked out, but I'm not about to let Reece get hauled off to prison, even if I don't understand what happened.

Frowning, John pulls a dishrag out of his pocket and furiously wipes his hands. He looks at me, eyes narrowed, studying me in a way that makes me want to squirm. I'm sure

I'm moments away from getting the boot, when he turns to the gorilla. "That *lunatic* over there"—he points at Reece— "is a decorated war hero. Any insult to him is an insult to me."

The man's eyes widen. "What? I didn't know—"

"Doesn't matter." John jabs a finger at the door. "Your patronage isn't welcome here. Please leave."

The guy opens his mouth to argue, but John cuts him off. "Leave. Before I *do* call the police."

Grumbling, the gorilla lumbers back to the door. He keeps his eyes locked on Reece the entire way.

When he's gone, John turns to the crowd. "Cannolis on the house. Please, everyone, return to your meals." He clasps a hand on my shoulder and steers me toward Reece, who's slumped against the wall, with his head held in his hands. "Let's go take care of our boy, eh?" he whispers.

My pulse thrums a steady beat inside my head. While Reece's behavior suddenly makes a lot more sense, I sure as hell don't know what to do about it. No matter what John said, he's definitely *not* my boy. Still, I allow John to steer me over to the corner.

Reece looks up. His eyes are more focused, but his shoulders continue to tremble. "God, John, I'm so sorry. I don't know what came over me. I—"

John waves the towel at him. "There's nothing to be sorry for."

"I need to go." Reece looks around the room, almost as if he's searching for something. "I need to go," he repeats.

"I know," John says. "And you can, but after you calm down a bit. Let's go in the kitchen. I'll make you a pie to go."

Reece doesn't move for several heartbeats. Finally, he gives a sharp nod.

John smiles and places his arm around his shoulder. "Good." He maneuvers Reece toward the swinging door, motioning me to follow with a wink and jut of his chin.

Honestly, I'm more than tempted to walk out the door and flag down a cab, call an Uber driver, or even jut my thumb out—whatever it takes to get the hell away from here. Yet I can't bring myself to abandon Reece. I've slipped out of dozens of beds the morning after without so much as a note good-bye. So, why now? What is it about Reece that I feel the need to stay and make sure he's okay?

With a sigh, I follow the two men beyond the swinging door. The smell of tomatoes, cheese, and garlic make me dizzy with hunger. We must be a sight to the half dozen employees kneading dough, sprinkling toppings, and shoving pizzas into and out of the large wood-burning ovens. But after their initial curious glances, they pay us no attention.

Which gets me wondering, has this happened before?

"I'm going to make you the usual, okay?" John steers us both to a corner with a single stool beneath a stainless steel table. He pulls the stool out and deposits Reece onto it. "Wait here, okay? Give me fifteen minutes. Both of you, relax."

He scuttles off, shouting orders to the workers while I shift my weight awkwardly from foot to foot. God, what sucky timing for me to give up drinking. I don't think I've ever needed a beer more than right now.

"I'm so sorry," Reece says, breaking through my thoughts. "This has really turned out to be some night out, huh?"

"Meh." I lift myself onto the table. "I've had worse nights. Besides, if this pizza is half as good as it smells, it just might make up for the near-brawl you dragged me into."

Reece gives me a crooked smirk. It dawns on me I don't think I've seen him smile before now. It looks good on him— really good.

"The food here is amazing," he confirms. "I've traveled the world, and nothing comes close to beating John's pizzas. He learned how to cook while stationed in Italy."

"Is that how you met?" I ask, swinging my legs.

"No. We met in group therapy." Reece looks away, making it obvious this isn't a conversation he wants to have.

I respect that, so I say nothing. After all, he hasn't asked about my car accident, drinking, or anything else, really. Since I already have to deal with my mother and brother—the two nosiest priers on the planet—it's nice to not have to get that deep into each other's business. Then again, I'm kind of a pro at the meaningless relationship.

This time it's my turn to look away.

"Again, I'm sorry this night took such a turn. After John comes back, I'll take you straight home."

That brings my attention back to him. "So you can eat the pizza without me? I don't think so, buddy."

He laughs. It's a nice sound that gives me a fluttery feeling in my stomach. That annoys me because I'm not thirteen. "Okay, fine," he says. "What do you propose?"

"I *propose* we go back to my apartment, turn on a movie, and eat the entire pizza, like damn adults. After which, I will gladly kick your ass to the curb."

He laughs again. "Actually, that sounds like a really good plan."

"Of course it is." I snort. "I came up with it. Just don't go all Jason Bourne on any of my neighbors—except the old perv who lives above me. I think he steals my Victoria's Secret catalogs. If you want to punch him in the face, that's totally fine with me."

He grins. "Old pervert. Check. Anything else I should know?"

"Let's see." I use my fingers to count off the list. "Share the pizza. Don't kill neighbors. Punch old perv. Ass kicked to the curb when done." I drop my hand into my lap. "That should cover it."

Folding his arms across his chest, he leans against the wall. "It sounds like this night might be salvageable, after all."

Chapter Ten

Reece

Emily's apartment is located in the historic part of downtown, only blocks away from the old capitol building. I park the bike in front of a dance studio. Emily smooths her skirt, and I pretend not to notice her mile-long legs as I unhook the bungee cords securing the pizza.

I have to admit, while I wasn't eager to go out tonight, it's been a damn interesting evening. And Emily is a damn interesting woman. What fascinates me most isn't the expanse of her legs or the curve of her breasts—though, I can't deny they aren't nice. It's the subtle things about her that intrigue me most—the slightly crooked tooth that's only visible when she laughs, the wicked arch of her eyebrow when she's pretending to be tough, and the fierceness in her eyes when she's afraid. Even when I'm the one who made her afraid.

Because I wasn't strong enough to fight off the fear. I'm starting to believe I never will be. Which is exactly why, even though I haven't been alone with a woman in years, this night can't go beyond friendly conversation and pizza.

Emily opens a blue paint-chipped door, revealing a hallway lined with green doors. Taking keys out of her clutch, she nods. "I'm the last door on the left."

My throat tightens as I hobble behind her. Anyone could be hiding behind those doors. They could have a gun, or — No. I shake my head. I might not be able to conquer my fear, but I can at least put it on hold for an hour.

She unlocks her door but pauses before opening it. With an arched eyebrow, the same one I've grown to enjoy, she asks, "What's up with your leg?"

So much for friendly conversation. "You're very subtle, you know that?"

She shrugs, takes the pizza box from me, and enters her apartment. After tossing the box on a coffee table, she flops down on a plush loveseat. "I don't believe in playing games. If I want to know something, I ask."

"Yeah, well I believe some shit should remain in the past where it belongs."

She shrugs again, kicks off her shoes, and snags a slice of pizza. A tendril of mozzarella slides off the crust. Emily quickly wraps it around her finger before popping it into her mouth.

I'm momentarily mesmerized by her sliding her finger out of her lips. I give myself a mental shake. Damn, it's been too long since I've been in the company of a woman.

"So what you're saying is," Emily continues, seemingly unaware of my momentary lapse into the land of impure thoughts, "the army really fucked you up, huh?"

With a sigh, I grab my own slice of pizza and sit in the recliner adjacent to her. "I'd rather not talk about my time in the army."

"Because it fucked you up." Her lips quirk smugly, and I suddenly have the intense desire to kiss them. The thought startles me so much, a bite of pizza gets lodged in my throat. I cough several times to work it free.

"I'll take that as a yes."

"You can take it any way you want."

"So, why won't you talk about it?"

God, she's annoyingly persistent. "Why don't we talk about you instead?"

"Fine." She bites into her pizza and holds her arms wide. "I'm an open book."

If this is a contest to see who can make the other uncomfortable, challenge accepted. "Who was that guy in the car accident with you?"

Swallowing, she rolls her eyes. "Some loser I picked up in a bar."

Her honesty catches me off guard. "You knew he was a loser and you picked him up anyway? Why the hell would you do that?"

She shoves a large chunk of crust into her mouth. "I guess it was a combination of boredom and feeling sorry for myself."

"And you were feeling sorry for yourself because…"

She huffs, and I fight to keep the grin off my face. "I don't know. Maybe because I'm a loser, too." She crams the last bit of crust into her mouth and chews angrily.

Huh. I lean back in the chair. I guess she wins this one. She really is an open book. "Sure you're not exaggerating?"

"Nope." She grabs another slice and tears into it. "I totally am. If you don't believe me, ask my mother."

I laugh.

"What's so funny?"

"I'm just surprised we have so much in common. If we're going by the opinions of our mothers, I guess that makes me a loser, too."

She snorts. "Yeah, like I'm going to buy that. You practically walked off a J.Crew ad."

I grunt. "Cute. You always judge people by their appearances?"

"*No.*" She sets the pizza down. "I'm *judging* you based on the facts. You have a degree and a full-time job. If I had either of those things, my mother would throw a fucking parade in my honor."

"If you ask *my* mother," I tell her, "she'd say I don't have the *right* degree or the *right* job."

Emily wrinkles her nose. I can't help but notice how adorable it makes her look. "That's stupid."

I shrug.

"What's the *right* job?" she asks.

"She wanted me to be a lawyer like her, my father, and my sister. A high school teacher is a little too mundane for her taste."

Emily tucks her legs beneath her. "So, if your family was so against it, why *did* you decide to become a teacher?"

"A bunch of reasons," I answer. "I guess I initially fell in love with the idea of making a difference. Of course, having the summers off to fish doesn't hurt, either. Anything was better than going to law school. I did all my fighting on the battlefield." What I don't tell her is that I'm still there, on those damn sandy dunes, every time I close my eyes.

Reflexively, I touch the bullet beneath my shirt.

Catching the movement, Emily's head tilts. "What's that?"

"A necklace." I cut her off before she can ask any more. "Tell me more about you. You are the open book, after all."

"Meh." She dusts her hands together. "My dad was a cop who died in the line of duty when I was little, hence the overbearing older brother you've apparently already met."

I nod. That explains her brother reaching for me in her hospital room.

"I'm a disappointment to my mother because I'm a 'barista with no future.'" She makes quotes with her fingers.

"Do you like being a barista?"

She makes a face. "Not really."

"Any idea what you might want to do?"

"I wish." She leans against the couch. "I'm not really cut out for college. And I'd rather stick a fork in my eye than be chained to a desk in some office."

We have something else in common. "Okay. So, you're still figuring it out."

She makes a face. "I guess. I spent the summer after my senior year traveling Europe. I thought that would be enough time to figure things out. Turns out, after two trips around the globe, I still haven't come up with a single thing."

"And you're how old?"

"Twenty-one."

I shake my head. "You still have a lot of time."

"Tell that to my mom."

"Parents are funny that way. If you deviate from the path they've chosen for you, you're automatically a failure. My mom and dad practically disowned me when I joined the army. We haven't spoken since I returned from my last tour."

"Why?"

"My dad told me it was a waste of my talent."

"That's harsh."

I give an angry laugh. "Maybe. But then again, maybe he was right. I wasn't a very good soldier."

"Because you got hurt?"

"No. Because I—" Realizing I'm on the verge of revealing too much, I quickly bite the words back. "Doesn't matter," I finally say.

She narrows her eyes, studying me as she chews. The intensity of her gaze makes my skin itch, and I'm desperate to shake it off. "What happened to the guy that was in the car accident with you?"

"Don't know." She sets her pizza down and brushes her

hands together. "And I don't care, either. Fucking asswipe."

"Sounds like it." I wonder if she knew the loser crawled away from the car, leaving her to die. Either way, I figure it's not worth mentioning.

"Like I said earlier," she continues, "I was bored and feeling sorry for myself." Grinning, she arches an eyebrow. "Sex is one of the few things that makes me forget about my pathetic life."

Her blunt admission startles me, but I fight to keep it from showing. I get this feeling Emily is toying with me, testing my reactions. I'm not sure if she's deliberately trying to push me away or if she's just this honest.

"You think that makes me a slut?"

"What I *think*," I counter, "is it's none of my business what you do for fun."

Still smiling, she stretches her feet onto the coffee table. Yup. Definitely toying with me. "It's nothing to be ashamed of."

"Didn't say that it was."

"It doesn't make me a slut."

"Didn't say it did."

"Girls can like sex just as much as guys." I can tell she's used to getting argued with on this point. The way she's leaning forward, eyes wide, shoulders tight, she's like a cat ready to pounce.

Regardless of what she's come to expect, she's not getting a fight from me. "I agree with you."

"Oh." She blinks several times before sinking back into the couch. It's almost as if she's disappointed I'm not challenging her.

"But just so you know," I continue, "you can't pigeonhole every guy, either. Some of us aren't obsessed with sex."

Her laugh comes out a snort. It's adorable. "Bullshit."

"You're calling me a liar?"

"Yup."

I hold my arms wide. "You're looking at one right here."

She laughs harder. "You're so full of shit."

"Fine." I grab another slice of pizza. "Believe what you want."

She watches me eat for several moments before blurting, "When's the last time you had sex?"

Shit. Good question. Mentally I tally the months in my head. The last woman I was with was my ex, Samantha. That was, shit, two…no, that's not right. "Three years ago," I answer.

Her eyes practically bulge from their sockets. "Why?"

I finish the last bite before answering. "Part of that time, I was in the desert. And the other part"—I shake my head—"I just haven't wanted to."

"You haven't wanted to?" She gives me a look as if I'd just admitted to performing ballet in my spare time. "Every guy wants to."

"Not me."

"Maybe that's why you're so strung out."

I can't help but laugh at that. "Maybe."

"A guy like you could get laid whenever he wanted, you know."

I make a face. "A crippled guy, with a teacher's salary. Yeah, I'm a real catch."

"No. The hot guy with the college degree and job with benefits. That guy can get laid."

"Did you just call me hot?"

Emily rolls her eyes. "Focus. What I'm saying is I think you should get out there and get some."

"And what I'm telling you is women equal drama. I don't need that in my life right now." I lift the pizza box lid, only to discover it's empty. I feel a pang of disappointment—not because I'm still hungry, but because I no longer have an excuse to hang out.

She studies me in that appraising way of hers. "Women don't always equal drama."

I snort. "Okay, let me rephrase: *sex* with women equals drama."

"You've obviously been hooking up with the wrong kind of girl. It is possible to have a good time with someone and leave it at that."

"Bullshit."

"Sex doesn't have to be complicated."

"Of course it does; it's sex. It's complicated physically and emotionally. That's the very nature of sex."

"Then you're doing it wrong," she argues.

"Or maybe you are."

She scowls at me, and little creased lines appear above her nose. Like everything else about her, they're adorable. And just as suddenly, the lines disappear as a smile stretches across her face. She stands, closing the distance between us in one stride. Before I realize what she's doing, she's straddles my lap, weaving her fingers behind my neck.

"The hell?" I try to stand, but my knee buckles.

"Relax." She laughs. I can't help but notice she smells amazing, something floral with a hint of musk. Her skin beneath my fingers is warm, soft. I forgot how good a woman feels in my grasp. Suddenly, I'm overcome with the urge to pull her against me. "I'm going to prove to you how uncomplicated this is."

"What do you mean *this*?" I have no clue what's going on. Ever since the war, I thought the part of me that craved physical touch was dead. But the longer Emily sits on my lap, the more I don't want to let her go.

She rolls her eyes. "Sex, dummy. But only if you want to. What do you say?"

"Huge mistake. Massive." I place my hands on her hips to ease her off me, but once my fingers settle in the curve of her waist, I find I no longer have control of them. I tighten my hold on her hips.

She grins, shifting her weight onto my lap. I grow hard beneath the thin layer of clothing separating us. "The only thing that was a mistake," she says, "was this disastrous fake date. We can, however, salvage the night." She leans forward, whispering beneath my ear, her words brushing velvet and hot against my skin. "What do you say? We have a little fun and then we both go on our merry way, never to harass one another again."

The Boy Scout in me wants to say no, but my mouth refuses to form the word. I'm practically aching for her. Luckily, my brain hangs on to some control. "It's never that simple. Whatever you need, I can't give it to you. I don't have my shit together enough for a relationship. I lost my ability to feel—*that way*—in the desert."

"A relationship?" She laughs. "That's the last thing I want."

"What *do* you want?"

"To take care of you." She breathes against my neck. My muscles coil tightly in response. "I think a single night of womanly attention would do you a world of good. Could be fun."

Twenty-four hours ago I never would have thought so. But now, my dick pulses with desire, something I haven't felt or even thought I'd feel ever again. That alone is enough to make me consider her offer. "I can't love you," I tell her. "I can't love anyone."

Her fingers wind up my neck, twisting into my hair. "I'm not asking you to."

God, she's soft. Have women always been this soft? I forgot. And she's gorgeous. She makes me feel things I thought I could no longer feel. Maybe I can do this, after all. I try to push the rising doubt from my head even as I untuck her shirt from her skirt and slide my hands up along her sides—the voice that reminds me it's been so long since I felt *anything,* there's no way I'll be able to satisfy a woman.

She moans and arches her back. Which gets me thinking, then again, maybe I do remember a thing or two. At this point, I can still muster the strength to walk away. But I can't guarantee I can if we go much further. "You really want to do this?" I need to hear her say it again, out loud,

With nimble fingers, she unbuttons my shirt before sliding her hands along my abs. "Oh yeah." Smiling, she sighs. "Absolutely. You?"

"Honestly, I can't remember the last time I've been sure about anything." She nibbles on my earlobe and I inhale sharply. I sure as hell didn't think I could feel that anymore.

"I'll be good to you," she says, pulling me closer, fingers twisting in my hair. "Just one night. Let me take care of you."

Take care of me, or prove once and for all how broken I am? I wonder, hands tightening on her waist. Either way, I've run out of excuses. "One night," I agree.

She leans back, grinning. God, she's so sexy, it's all I can do not to explode right now. It *has* been a very long time.

"I'm going to do you so good," she says, "you might regret only signing on for one night. Just wait until you see what you're going to lose."

This gives me pause, though I doubt it's for the reasons she wants. I've already lost so much—a brother-in-arms, a career, a kneecap…a life. And this girl thinks she's going to get to me? If anything, she's going to prove how little of me is actually left. "I think I'll get over it."

"We'll see." She tugs my shirt off and throws it across the room.

Maybe she didn't mean it, but I swear I heard the hint of a challenge in her voice. Still, I'm not afraid. If there's one thing I'm good at, it's not feeling a thing.

Chapter Eleven

EMILY

I run my hands over his chest. I don't need alcohol to make Reece look good. The muscles of his chest are hard under my fingers, his shoulders taught, his jaw strained. I have the sudden urge to scratch my nails down his back to find out how deep I have to go to get to something soft.

He grabs my waist tightly and tugs me against him so sharply, I gasp.

"I'm sorry." He immediately lets go and tries to gently push me off of him. "This was a mistake."

"I'm not sorry." I weave my fingers behind his neck and look at him. His lake blue eyes are wide with fear. He thinks he hurt me, I realize. "*Ohhhh.* I get it now."

He frowns, obviously not the reaction he expected.

"That's what's got you so messed up."

"What?"

"The shit that happened to you in the desert—you forgot how to be gentle, and you're scared you're going to hurt me."

He jerks back, as if considering this for the first time. "Maybe…"

"You won't," I cut him off.

He doesn't look convinced.

"I might not be a badass soldier like you, Reece, but I think you'll find I'm not easily broken." This time I don't fight my urges and dig my nails into his back.

A rumbling growl emits from deep inside his chest. He grasps my hips and leans forward, trailing his lips up my collar bone, to the dip in my shoulder and then up my neck. When he gets to the tender skin beneath my jaw, the warm velvet of his lips is replaced by the sharp heat of teeth.

I gasp as the flash of pain quickly turns to waves of desire.

He leans back, worry evident on his face. "Did I hurt you?"

I smile. "Oh, honey, you're going to have to try harder than that."

He groans, a primal sound that tightens things low inside me. He slides a finger into my hair and curls his fingers into a fist before tilting my head back sharply, inclining my neck. "Don't tempt me."

Every nerve in my body sizzles with need. I whimper, which, in turn, makes him smile. Holy hell, I think I finally found a guy who can keep up with me.

With my hair firmly ensnared in his hand, he grazes his teeth down my neck. Gasping, I reach for his pants buckle. He catches my hands before I can fumble the button open.

"No," he orders. "It's been a long time. A really long time. I want to make this last, and if you touch me right now, I won't be able to."

I open my mouth to protest, but he covers my lips with his. His mouth is so hot, his tongue so urgent, I can feel myself melting into the kiss. Melting, and melting, until I'm sure he's going to devour me whole.

I'm limp in his arms when he finally releases me. He licks his lips. "God, you taste good."

"I feel good, too," I say, between gasps for air.

Something dark flashes through his eyes. "You need to let me know if things get too...intense."

"I already told you—"

"I know what you told me," he cuts me off. "You still need to tell me."

I make a face. "Like a safe word or something?"

His eyes narrow. "No safe word. Just tell me to stop, and I'll stop. It's that simple."

This seems really important to him, so I don't bother to argue. Instead, I lick my lips. "Okay."

As soon as the word leaves my mouth, he grasps my shirt with his free hand, and rips it open. He still hasn't let go of my hair, leaving me ensnared.

"I'll pay for that," he says, while appraising my breasts. The hunger in his eyes makes me squirm with need. His dick, so hard beneath me, pulses in response.

"Don't worry. I'll make sure you do." I slide my hips forward, grinding against the bulge of his jeans.

Growling, he yanks down my bra. My breasts spill over the black lacy fabric. My nipples are already tight with need, so when he takes one into his mouth and sucks hard, it's all I can do not to buck against him. Strings of desire lace from my nipples to the spot low inside me, forming a web that he pulls tighter with each swipe of his tongue.

Finally, he tilts his head back and groans. "You are..." He shakes his head. "It's like you're too good to be true. You're beautiful, you're sexy, you're...not afraid."

"I'm not."

"Maybe you should be." He meets my eyes. "Fear strips your humanity. It makes you an animal. I *feel* like an animal."

"Then be an animal."

Releasing my hair, he flips me over onto the couch without warning. I barely have time to yelp before he's behind me, straddling me. He grabs my hips, fingers digging into my skin so hard, I'm sure I'll be bruised tomorrow.

And that makes me crazy with need. The flashes of pain don't last long before they turn into explosions of desire. Maybe there's something not right about me, but I've always preferred my sex rough. Up until this point, I've never had a man strong enough to give me exactly what I've craved. Now, however, I think I've met my match.

Just the thought that tomorrow I've have actual *marks* from this man, that I'll have evidence he claimed me as his, that he *owned me*, is enough to build the pressure between my legs to an almost explosion.

Leaning over me, he grabs my breasts with his hands, squeezing, as his breath runs hot trails down my neck. The bulge, contained only by his jeans, slams against my sweet spot, again and again, leaving me squirming and desperate.

"Please," I pant.

He grows still. For one terrifying moment, I'm afraid he's changed his mind. But then he pushes my skirt up to my waist and slides my panties down to my ankles.

A high desperate mewl escapes my throat. I'm throbbing with a need so strong, it aches.

There's a rustling of fabric, the unmistakable sound of cellophane followed by the snap of a condom being pulled into place.

I almost groan in relief.

He leans over me and bites my ear once before whispering, "Tell me you want this. Tell me you want *me*." The tip of his penis grazes my skin.

Crazy with desire, I thrust back, but he catches my hips, stopping me. "Tell me, first."

I don't hesitate. "I want you." My voice quivers with

desire. "I want you so bad."

He slams into me without warning. There's no gentle glide, or feeling me out. He's just there, filling me up, hitting the spot inside me that makes my eyelids flutter, and then he's gone again, leaving me empty and desperate.

I wriggle backward, dying to have him back inside me, when he forces my hips still.

"Emily"—his voice is thick with hunger—"it's been so damn long. I...I just don't know if I can make it last."

My chest is heaving, my breasts bobbing, nipples painfully tight. "If you can't make it last, at least make it count."

His hips slam into me in response. His dick throbs with need with each thrust. The soft tip of it hits the spot just below my navel, filling my hidden cup with pulsing warm honey. Again, and again, until I can't contain it anymore and it spills over the sides.

Throwing my head back, I cry out as spools of pleasure unravel from my core, spiraling down into my fingers and toes. Electricity buzzes through my veins, igniting everything in its path until I'm consumed by it.

His thrusts continue to pound in time with my pulses until another wave builds. He winds his fingers into my hair and pulls tight.

That's all it takes to send me over the edge. Again.

A first for me.

I'm still crying out from the first orgasm when the spasms inside me renew in strength. My entire body bucks as tremors seize me.

Behind me, Reece grunts, and his bucking slows from a steady rhythm into uneven thrusts. Letting go of my hair, he places both hands on my hips and thrusts one last time, pulling me against him as he does.

As my own spasms die down, I can feel his dick tremble inside me.

Reece gasps and loosens his hold on me.

I collapse on the couch. He falls beside me.

"That was...insanely amazing," I pant.

"Did I hurt you?" The worry is evident in his voice. "I'm so sorry—"

"Don't you dare." I sit up, remove my panties from my ankles, and smooth my skirt down. "That was, literally, the best sex of my life."

He makes a face. "It wasn't very long. And if I hurt you—"

Sighing, I pull my bra back into place. "I told you I like it rough. I would have let you know if you crossed the line."

He stares at me a moment before nodding. "All right." He slides his jeans up, and I grab his hand, stopping him. "What are you doing?" he says.

"I'm just thinking, if that was the best sex I ever had, and it was that fast, imagine what the next round is going to be like."

"Next round?" He quirks an eyebrow.

"Or third. Or fourth. They can only get better, right? Science, Reece. We must solve this mystery for science."

He grins. "Well, I am a teacher. I do love learning." He leaves his button open wide. "All right, let's do this. For science."

Chapter Twelve

Can't sleep.

Reece snores peacefully beside me. Even though my body feels like a combination of melted butter and sore satisfaction, my stupid brain refuses to shut the fuck up.

Another notch on the ol' bedpost, huh? Wonder what your mother would think of that—or your brother, for that matter. Don't you have more self-respect than this? Don't you have any aspirations at all?

"Damn it," I mutter, throwing the covers back. So much for enjoying the afterglow—and this one takes the cake. Usually now is when would I sneak out of bed and dress with ninja stealth. Or, since this is my apartment, this would be the time I plant an elbow in the guy's ribs and make some excuse for needing to be up early in the morning.

I glance at Reece, his arm flung over his face and his chest rising and falling in a peaceful rhythm. God, he's so much fun to look at. I can't bring myself to wake him. "Fuck," I whisper, digging my palms into my eyes. I don't know what it is about this guy, but he gets under my skin, makes me soft.

I don't like it.

The sooner he's out of my bed—out of my *life*—the better. For now, I need to get away from him before my damn hormones get the better of me again. I silently climb out of bed, snag a pair of underwear and a cami off my dresser, and head to the kitchen.

I grab my phone off the counter. I've received over a dozen texts from Ash and Lane. Ash wants to know how my date went, while Lane wants to make sure I didn't fall off the wagon.

I roll my eyes as I set the phone aside. Looks like overprotective Lane is back. Still, I have to admit, a drink sounds really fucking good right about now.

I stare longingly at the empty space above the fridge where I used to keep my bottle of whiskey. "Damn it," I whisper. Without booze, I'm not sure how to quiet the whispers of self-loathing.

Because you're an alcoholic, the voice reminds me. *A pathetic loser alcoholic.*

I fling the kitchen cabinet wide, searching for any bottles I might have missed—the nasty, fruity wine I received as a Christmas gift last year, the cupcake vodka Ashlyn brought over on our last movie night, even the Irish crème left over from last Christmas. Gone. All of it dumped down the drain by my own traitorous hands.

All of it except...

I fling the cabinet above the sink open, grab the cough syrup, and unscrew the cap with shaking fingers. The moment the bottle touches my lips, Reece grunts from my bedroom and I freeze. Is he awake? Did he see me?

Slowly I turn in the direction of my open bedroom door. He tosses on the bed, burying his face into the pillow. He snorts before going still.

My muscles unwind and I lower the bottle. *What the hell am I doing?* I place the cough syrup back inside the cabinet and rake my fingers through my tangled hair. *Get it together, Em. You're better than this.*

I inhale deeply. On the refrigerator is a magnet my mom gave me when I started A.A. I'm supposed to read it when I feel tempted or some shit. Desperate times and all. I walk to the fridge and read.

God, grant me the serenity to accept the things I cannot change, the courage to change the things I can, and the wisdom to know the difference.

Pretty words, I think, chewing on my lip. But what if it's *me* that can't be changed?

No. I refuse to think like that. It's courage I need. Change.

But just thinking about change, and wishing for it, doesn't make it happen. The need for a drink twists around my body like barbed wire. Squeezing. Cutting.

I rack my brain, trying to remember the things I did to cope before I turned to alcohol. I used to call my friends. But that was in high school before they all left for college and outgrew me. I used to get inked. There's something about the rush of a needle digging into your skin that makes you forget all about your problems. Too bad there's not a tattoo shop open at this hour.

A memory surfaces from a dark, dusty corner of my brain. It slams into me with enough force that I stagger back against the counter. After Dad died, I stayed with Grandma for a week while Mom and Lane arranged Dad's funeral. The first night I couldn't fall asleep in the cold, strange bed. So, Grandma took me downstairs to the kitchen, turned on the oven and pulled out bowls, spoons, and measuring cups. We baked everything from honey bread to cookies. We baked coffee cake and pie, *kugelis* and casseroles. We baked until the sun bled through the windows and every inch of the counter space was covered by a mountain of baked goods—enough to feed an entire city, let alone a funeral.

Even the chairs were piled with casserole dishes. After the last muffin was pulled from the oven, Grandma and I sat on the sugar-covered floor, sticky and exhausted. She held me against her, and I was finally able to cry.

But I survived.

If I could survive the death of my father, I sure as hell can survive this, too.

Opening the cabinets, I pull out bags of flour, sugar, and baking powder. I can't remember the last time I used any of it. Does sugar expire? Muttering a silent prayer that I won't kill anyone with food poisoning, I scoop out a cup of flour and level it with a knife.

Slowly, like grains of flour falling from a sifter, Grandma's baking recipes return to me. Our baking together didn't end at Dad's funeral. From that day on, any time I visited her house, we would bake something, usually because I demanded it. She taught me the importance of room temperature eggs and butter, and how to whip frosting to the consistency of clouds. We baked bread from her homeland of Lithuania as well as American favorites, like cupcakes and chocolate chip cookies.

Taste everything, Emily, she had said during a baking session. *Experiment and modify to your tastes. It might be awful, but you also might stumble upon something amazing. A real baker bakes with her heart, never a recipe book.*

So I did. In the beginning, I made some awful things. But gradually, I got the hang of it, and even became good at it.

I dip my finger into the batter and lick it. *I'm still good at it,* I think with a smile.

So why the hell did I stop?

I grab the wooden spoon and resume stirring, realizing I'm literally holding on to the answer. *Grandma's spoon.* In fact, almost every bowl, measuring cup, baking dish, and cookie sheet I own was hers. I received them all after Grandma died nearly six years ago. I stopped because it reminded me too much of her.

"I don't think I've ever said this out loud, but I miss you," I whisper to the ceiling. "And Daddy, too," I add, because I don't want him to feel left out. I know it's stupid, talking to the ceiling, but holding Grandma's spoon, I can almost smell her lilac perfume in the kitchen with me.

The oven dings, pulling me from my thoughts. After lining a muffin tin with paper cups, I fill them with batter and slide the tray into the oven. I set the timer and then start on the frosting.

Fifteen minutes later, the timer goes off. Opening the oven door fills the kitchen with the aroma of butter and vanilla.

Electricity dances along my spine. Damn. I forgot how much I love this. I'm way too excited to sleep now, so I make a cup of coffee and wait for the cupcakes to cool.

While I lean against the counter, sipping my coffee, I can feel her standing beside me like she did ten years ago, smiling at me. Encouraging me. Reminding me I once had potential.

And maybe I still do.

Chapter Thirteen

The blast sets my ears ringing and floods my vision with spots. Even through the whine of my aching ear drums, I can hear his screams.

Chad.

I push to my feet and try to run to him. But the sand won't let me. The same goddamn sand that scratches my eyes, coats my throat, and covers every inch of my skin. My legs sink up to my knees, making each step forward a battle in itself.

"Chad." I try to scream his name, but the wind kicks up, carrying my voice away and filling my throat with more shit-flavored dust, until I can't breathe. I cough, choke, and claw at my throat with blood-crusted fingernails.

Chad.

His screams go quiet.

My heart slams against my ribs, threatening to burst through my chest. *No. Not again.*

An arm shoots out of the dune beside my leg. The sleeve

is distinctly military camo, but the hand at the end is skeletal. It snatches at my thigh, twisting into the fabric and ripping it with bony fingers.

The first arm is followed by a second, then a third. Suddenly several burst through the sand all at once, each clawing at my legs, pulling me deeper into the ground.

Burying me with them.

I struggle, kicking, thrashing, but it's no good. The skeletal fingers only yank me down faster. They drag me deeper until I'm up to my waist in sand, then my neck, until it's at my mouth, filling my throat, drowning my screams.

"Reece!"

My eyes fly open.

I'm in the dark, legs restrained. I fight and kick, even with my bum knee throbbing, to get the ropes off me. Only when my hands find them, I realize it's not ropes holding me captive, but a sheet twisted around my ankles.

"Reece?" A woman's voice. *That's new.*

I turn toward the sound and find her standing in the doorway. Blonde. Tattooed.

Wait. Not *just* a woman. A really sexy blonde in a tank top and lace panties. *Emily,* the name flashes in my mind.

Slowly, the pieces fall into place. I'm not under attack. I'm at Emily's apartment. I think we had sex.

No, wait.

We *definitely* had sex.

Really amazing sex.

Damn.

I suck in a ragged breath as I unwind the sheet from my legs.

"Nightmare?" She hugs her arms across her chest.

I ignore her question. Questions lead to talking, and talking brings back the past. I'm haunted enough without willingly seeking out my demons. I swing my legs over the side of the bed. "I should go."

Something dark passes through her eyes—barely a glimmer—and it's gone before I can decipher it. "Yeah, probably." She's silent a moment then shrugs. "But there's no hurry."

The need to get back to the familiarity of my own house has me practically twitching. I force myself to dress slowly. We both agreed nothing would come out of our night together. Still, I don't want to be the kind of asshole who screws a girl and then leaves a cloud of dust in his wake.

I scan the room for my jeans and find them strewn halfway across the floor. My cane is a good several feet away. *Shit.* I hate people seeing me limp.

It makes me weak.

Vulnerable.

"Would you mind?" I nod to my jeans.

She gives another shrug and pushes off the doorframe. "Sure." She picks up my jeans and walks them over to me, hesitating, with her arm held out. "That sure is one hell of a nasty scar you got there." She nods at the jagged pink line across my knee.

Ignoring her comment, I snatch my pants from her grip. "Thanks."

She turns her gaze to the mangled bullet hanging at my neck. Her eyes widen. "Where did you get that?"

"The desert," I mutter, fighting the urge to flinch from the pain searing up my leg as I pull on my jeans.

"Was that—was that—inside you?"

"Nope." I fasten the button.

"So how did you get it?"

I grunt and meet her eyes. She sure asks a lot of questions for someone who promised no strings attached. "You know you're not supposed to ask a soldier about what happened in the desert, right? It summons the demons."

She opens her mouth to answer. Before she can, I notice something else different about the apartment. There's a heavy scent wafting through the doorway. Sugary. Buttery. Warm.

"Have you been baking?" I ask.

She levels my gaze with her own. "Yeah. So?"

"At four in the morning?"

"I couldn't sleep."

I don't challenge that. I can certainly relate.

"That reminds me. Don't leave just yet, okay?" She disappears, only to reappear seconds later with a cupcake in her hands. "Would you try this for me? It's been ages since I made anything, and I'm not sure I got the recipe just right."

"Uh, sure." I run my hands through my sweat-damp hair. Sex and cupcakes? I mean, sure, it's been a long time since I got laid, but this can't be normal.

She hands me the yellow cupcake piled high with vanilla frosting and then steps back. Watching me, she knots her fingers together, biting on her bottom lip.

I'll be damned, I think, as I peel the paper cup back. *This tough-as-nails girl is actually nervous.* I cross my fingers that the cupcake is good. I'd hate to let her down, and I'm a terrible liar.

Turns out, I didn't have to worry.

As soon as I bite into it, I'm rendered speechless by the taste of buttery cake and sugar. "Oh my God," I mumble with my mouth full.

She grins, bouncing on her toes like a child. "That means you like it, right? You like it?"

I nod and take another bite. "This is the best thing I've put in my mouth, ever.

She gets a devilish grin. "Really? *Ever?*"

I know she's implying what happened last night. I can't help it, I grin back. "Well, almost ever." I pop the rest of the cupcake into my mouth. "Did you find that recipe on Pinterest or something?"

"Oh hell no." She jerks back. "That's a secret recipe straight from my Grandma."

"She was smart to keep it secret." I fold the wrapper into a small square. "If the world knew about these, there would be wars fought over them."

Her grin widens. "I'll get you another one." She bounds off and returns a moment later with another cupcake in hand. This one is chocolate with chocolate frosting.

"You made two different kinds? How long was I asleep?"

"I went a little overboard," she says, handing me the cupcake. "It's better than drinking."

I tip the cupcake in agreement.

She sits beside me on the bed, swinging her legs. "You don't drink, do you?"

Shaking my head, I bite into the cupcake. Just like the one before, this one dissolves in my mouth. Good thing we agreed this was a one-time thing. This girl and her baking skills would be murder on my workout regime. "I haven't touched alcohol since the night before I left for the desert."

She frowns. "So how do you deal with—you know?" She nods at me, as if my PTSD were an infection covering my entire body. Actually, I realize, that's not an inaccurate assessment. "Did they give you pills or something?"

"I have pills for when things get bad."

Her eyes widen. "Tonight wasn't bad?"

"Last night was a vacation in the Bahamas compared to bad." I got to hand it to her, this girl knows how to get me talking. I shove the rest of the cupcake into my mouth and reach for my shoes.

Emily watches me without a word as I get dressed, even hands me my cane when I'm finished. Once I'm on my feet, I realize just how heavy the awkwardness between us has become. It settles on my shoulders, thick and hot, like a wet towel pulled too-soon from the dryer. I rub the back of my neck. I'm itching to flee, but I'm not sure how to make the first move. "So I guess I'll—"

"Don't," she says cutting me off.

"Don't what?"

She grunts. "Don't say you'll call me or you'll see me around. Don't feed me any lines. We both know what last night was—two consenting adults having a bit of fun."

I nod, even though at the time it felt so much more than that. "Right. Fun."

She sits there, perched on the end of her bed, swinging her legs. I'm desperate to return to a familiar setting, my safe place, but she looks so vulnerable right now. I want to take her in my arms and hold her against me.

But that wasn't part of the deal.

I swallow hard. "I'm gonna get going."

She nods, glancing at the floor before meeting my eyes. "You know, Reece, you're not as stuffy and uptight as I thought you were."

I chuckle. "Thanks? You're not as loud and obnoxious as I thought you were."

She laughs before falling quiet. After a brief silence she says, "I'm glad we did this. It was bizarre, awkward, and I thought we might be going to jail for a minute there. Still, I had fun."

"Me, too." Though, I'm not sure fun is the right word to describe it. Last night, when I held her in my arms, a piece of myself I thought was dead and gone returned to life.

"Promise me one thing, Reece?" She tilts her head to the side.

"What's that?"

"Don't be a stranger, okay? Maybe we can exchange numbers?"

I nod, even as I study every line of her body, trying to

commit it to memory. I want to remember how she is in this moment—messy hair, no makeup, and smelling of sugar. I want to remember her, because I, the Boy Scout, lied. I won't be dropping by her apartment, and I won't be calling. As amazing as she is, she's too dangerous to be around.

In the military, we're trained to survive. Last night, this woman found a way through to my humanity, but I'll be damned if I let her into my heart—whatever little there is left of it.

Chapter Fourteen

Emily is all I can think about. Her smell. The feel of her body. The sound of her laugh. The way I claimed her when she was beneath me — for that brief moment, she was mine. And now, she's another ghost I'm cursed to have haunt me. It's my own damn fault for letting my guard down.

So damn weak.

The following Monday, I avoid the coffee shop where Em works. When I walk into school without my usual cup, Tonya questions me. I tell her I didn't have time to stop, even though I made it to school thirty minutes early.

I avoid Em's coffee shop again the next day, and the day after that. I tell Tonya the tar-like coffee at the chain place is so much better. She always answers with a skeptical look, but she never questions me. How can I admit to Tonya — or to *myself* — that it feels like the tattooed barista somehow unzipped my skin and wriggled her way inside? The more I think about Emily, the more terrified I become.

And I was already a terrified mess before she asked me out on that fake date. If she has me this messed up after one night together, I sure as hell can't risk anymore. I want her out of my head. If that means playing the asshole, I guess that's the role I'll have to take.

Self-preservation. It's what soldiers do. No matter how much it hurts.

The days of avoiding Emily turn into weeks, and the weeks stretch into a month. I still feel that little tug inside trying to pull me in the direction of the coffee shop every time I drive past. But every day that passes, every hour, every minute, our night together fades just a fraction more, loosening Em's hold over me.

But it's still not enough.

I'm pacing my apartment like a caged lion, even after riding my bike for an hour. Not even Sheila can lessen the itch this time. Anxiety buzzes beneath my skin like an electric current. For the first time in my life, I wish I drank. I'm on the verge of a bad attack. I can feel it rolling closer like the charge before a storm.

There's only one thing that can help me when I get this bad.

The lake.

Too bad it's a Thursday and I have class in the morning.

I'm desperate. Sometimes just getting ready for a fishing weekend is enough to calm my nerves.

I open my closet, grab my tackle box, and settle onto the couch. I have a couple fishing lures that could use a little tweaking. Unfortunately, after rummaging through my box, my needle nose pliers are nowhere to be found.

Damn it. I bet I left them on the shore, which means they're long gone now. I slam the lid closed and snatch my keys off the coffee table.

With nothing better to do, and in desperate need of a

distraction, it looks like it's off to the hardware store I go. There's a small, locally owned place not even five minutes from my house. Since I haven't eaten, I can grab a sandwich on the way back and make a night of it.

I wonder how pissed Chad would be if he knew the sad, pathetic life he died saving. I bet if it were the other way around, he'd be graduated from the veterinary school he was always going on about and well on his way to saving puppies and kittens. Just thinking about it makes me clench my teeth together so hard my jaw aches.

What a fucking waste.

When I arrive at the hardware store, it takes me a minute to locate the pliers. The local place is quite a bit smaller and definitely more unorganized than the big chain stores. The ceiling is low, and the aisles narrow—too narrow. Anyone could be hiding around the corner, and I wouldn't be able to spot them until too late.

The second the thought crosses my mind, my heart starts with palpitations, signaling an oncoming panic attack. There's an abandoned cardboard box lying on the ground. It's the perfect size to hold a bomb.

My palms slicken with sweat.

Down the aisle a way, a guy in ripped jeans examines the boxes of conduits. His boots are dirty, his fingers stained. He's probably a contractor, electrician, or plumber. Even as my palms grow sweaty and my throat tightens, I watch him with growing envy. I bet he didn't even look twice at the fucking cardboard box. Why would he?

Jealously rolls through my veins fire-hot. What I wouldn't give to trade lives with him. To have an existence where nobody's ever tried to kill me, where dead bodies weren't a daily occurrence, and where I never watched a good man be murdered in front of me.

Something clatters an aisle away, making me jerk flat

against the shelves. Overhead the lights glow brighter and brighter until they become the sun itself, reflecting off of mountains of sand. A dust storm swirls around, rubbing grit into my skin. Sand coats my throat.

In the distance I hear a crash. Or is it an explosion? Before I can investigate, a bullet whizzes past my hair, so close it ruffles my hair.

I flatten myself against a boulder.

"Not real," I murmur. "Not real. Not real. Not real."

In the distance I hear screams. *Chad's screams.*

A sob swells up my throat, and I quickly swallow it down. I've been trained too well to let my emotions get the best of me and give away my position. For once I think about doing the opposite. I consider screaming at the top of my lungs loud enough for every damn fucker in the entire desert to find me.

At least then it would be over.

And that's what I want more than anything.

When I'm praying in bed. When I'm running from my ghosts. When I'm back in the desert.

Please God, just let it be over.

Chapter Fifteen

EMILY

I can't believe I actually thought for a millisecond J.Crew would be any different. Even more baffling, I can't believe I wanted him to be.

The day after Reece spent the night, Ashlyn called begging for details from our date. Of course I gave her the fluff version; we ate pizza, we talked, it ended. I sure as hell wasn't going to tell her I slept with him. Ash would never tell me she disapproved of some of my choices, but I could always hear it in her voice. And sleeping with a guy on the first date would guarantee a one-syllable "Oh," so heavy with disappointment it would practically ooze out my end of the phone.

But I'm not disappointed. And I don't regret it. Sex with Reece, while so damn hot, was also something *more*. And while I can't come up with what exactly that *more* is, I can admit that stupid, stupid boy left an impression.

I can't stop thinking about him.

And that pisses me off.

Usually with a guy, I'm out the door before my orgasm is even done pulsing, never to be seen again. And I'm good with that because it works. It keeps things simple. Neat.

But there's nothing simple about Reece "Monsieur Asswipe" Garrett.

Because that fucker ruined casual sex for me.

For the first time in my life, I'm craving seconds, and I can't figure out why.

Maybe he's just different enough to be interesting. On some level, despite our differences, we make a weird kind of sense. He's damaged; I'm damaged. He has issues with his parents. I have issues with my mother. He doesn't believe in relationships. I—don't even know anymore.

Because he got to me.

And I hate myself for letting him. Caring makes me one of *those girls*—the kind Ren and I make fun of. The first couple days after our night together, I found myself spending my coffee shop shifts watching the door, impatient for him to come in and order his usual Americano.

The second week, I kept my phone in my apron, set to vibrate, so I wouldn't miss his call.

The third week, I entered his name into every social media site.

Nothing. Nothing. And more nothing.

The man slept with me, and he disappeared.

I can't fault him for it. I more or less told him to. Still, I'll be damned if it didn't hurt. At first, the pain was more interesting than alarming. I honestly believed I couldn't be hooked by a guy—especially not one as straight-laced as J.Crew. When weeks stretched into a month, my self-exploratory interest waned, replaced by honest to God pain.

Which doesn't make sense. Yeah, our night together was fucking amazing, but it wasn't like I'd fallen in love with him or anything. So why did I let it get to me when he never called?

Why, after grabbing a burger from the drive-thru, did I turn my car around when I spotted his bike in the hardware store parking lot? Why did I park my car, walk into the store, and am now wandering the aisles looking for him, when I have no idea what to say?

Because you're a fucking idiot, the voice in my head answers back.

I really, really am.

I turn the corner down the paint aisle. He's not there. My confidence wavers, but I continue on. I can do this. I *have* to do this. I need to prove to myself he's nothing special and then purge him from my system. When I find him, I'll give him the proper dismissal he deserves.

I wonder if he'll make up some lame excuse, or pretend not to recognize me. Either reaction will be fine. It'll prove he's a dick just like all the rest, and then I can move on.

I bet he's not even as hot as I remember.

I trudge down aisle after aisle. No Reece.

My heart sinks into my knees. I need to find him so I can get over this stupid infatuation and get back to my life.

And then I do find him.

I turn down the very last aisle and find him crouched against shelves of PVC pipe. His eyes have the same wild look in them that they did the night we were at the pizza place. He's looking at me in that unfocused way; I know he's looking through me. He's gripping the shelf behind him so hard, his knuckles are white.

If I was looking for a sign that Reece Montgomery is a man I don't want in my life, this is it. I don't have to have a psychology degree to know this guy is seriously fucked in the head. If I had any sense at all, I'd turn around, go home with my burger, and forget I ever met him.

But like my mom says, I've never been one for common sense.

Chapter Sixteen

Heart hammering, I spin, preparing myself to dive for cover, only to smack into a warm body. I cry out, raising my hands, preparing to fight.

"You're okay." A familiar voice cuts through my panic. "Everything is okay."

It's Emily. Or at least I think it is. The sand recedes, leaving the hardware store in its place. But no matter how many times I blink, my eyes refuse to bring her shape into focus. "Tell me it's you." I raise a hand to touch her cheek. Her skin is warm and soft.

She flinches before stepping back, letting my hand fall. She doesn't want me touching her. Can't say I blame her, but what surprises me is how it makes my heart twist.

"It's happening again, isn't it?" she asks.

I pinch the bridge of my nose. "It's fine. I'm fine."

"You look like shit."

Her blunt honesty makes me crack a smile and brings

the world around me into sharper focus. "Probably. You look great." I say this in hope of changing the subject, but that doesn't make it any less true. Her signature red bandana, the same color as her lipstick, holds back her curls, while the neckline of her black blouse reveals the lacy edge of a red bra beneath.

This time when my throat tightens, fear has nothing to do with it. "So, how have you been?"

"Reece, please." Em rolls her eyes. "You don't have to do this. I just wanted to make sure you're okay."

"Don't have to do *what*?"

She huffs. "The small talk thing."

"Isn't that what people are supposed to do?" Just having her here beside me, pissed and all, slows my pulse and loosens my chest. Finally, I can breathe.

"Small talk is for relatives, friends, and acquaintances. We're none of the above, and that's okay."

"Ouch."

Her brow furrows. "I'm not trying to hurt you. It's what we both wanted." She angles her chin high, daring me to disagree. For someone who claims not to care, her wide stance and tight shoulders tell a different story.

Guilt snakes through my gut. "Look, I'm sorry—"

"Stop. I don't want your apology." She places a hand against her forehead. "I just want...closure."

"Closure? I don't have a clue what the hell you're talking about."

Leaning against a shelf, she lets out a long breath. "I need to know you're an ass, that you're just like all the rest."

I jerk back. "You need to know *what*?"

"You used to come to the coffee shop every morning. We sleep together, and suddenly you vanish."

Shame burns sour on the back of my tongue. "You told me you didn't want strings."

"Exactly," she continues. "So why haven't I seen you at the coffee shop? Do you have a girlfriend or—" Her eyes widen. "Oh, God. Are you *married*?"

I nearly choke. "I'm *not* married."

For some reason, she looks disappointed by my admission. "Oh. I was hoping—" Tugging on a curl, she bites off the rest of her words. Her gaze drops to the floor. "Never mind. You probably think I'm crazy, and you wouldn't be far off. I know I said no strings, but I've been thinking about you. Way more than I should." She swallows hard. "God, I'm an idiot. Can you forget this encounter ever happened?"

She turns to leave, and I reach out and snag her wrist. Maybe it's her sudden vulnerability, or the fact I've felt the same, but I can't hold the truth in any longer. "You're right. I've been avoiding you."

"Thank God." Her shoulders droop and she exhales slowly. "You *are* a jackass. That's exactly the closure I was looking for."

"You're not even giving me a chance to explain?" I scowl.

"You don't have to. I get it. And now I can move on."

I give a frustrated growl. "God, you're *impossible,* you know that? You act like you have it all figured out, but the truth is you don't know a damned thing."

Her eyes widen and she wrenches free from my grasp. "And you do?"

"More than you."

Her mouth drops and she makes a small, choking sound.

I enjoy the silence for all five seconds of it. Something tells me it's a rare occurrence.

She snaps her mouth shut and places a hand on her hip. "All right then, Mr. Teacher Man, if I'm so fucking clueless, fill me in. Tell me the real reason you stopped coming around."

Shit. I walked right into that one. Still, she's pushed too far for me to back down now. "Have it your way. Let's do this.

Yes, I've been avoiding you, but it's not for the reason you think."

"Ha." Her laugh hits me in the gut like a punch. "Oh, please do enlighten me."

The sarcasm in her voice ignites my blood, heating the words on my tongue. "It's true, I barely know you. What I do know is you are a fucking coward. You may act all tough and shit, but the truth is you're afraid of everything."

Her cheeks burn crimson. "That's bullshit."

"Is it? You were whining about having no direction in life, but you're too afraid to make a decision."

"Whining?" The flush bleeds into her neck.

"You're scared of relationships, of growing up, and starting an adult life. So you hit the pause button and feel sorry for yourself when the world passes you by."

"You've got a lot of nerve, asshole—"

"But I don't," I cut her off. "I'm just as big of a coward. I'm afraid each time I leave the house. I'm afraid of living a life I don't deserve. And I'm afraid of opening myself up to someone, only to find out that everything inside of me died in the desert."

She blinks, remaining silent.

"Look, Em, I'm sorry. I'm not cut out for the casual thing. I haven't been able to stop thinking about our night together—about you. And that scares the shit out of me more than anything. Because I can't do a relationship, either. I don't have it in me to give a woman what she needs."

Emily makes a face. "I don't understand you. Why does everything have to be so black and white?"

"Why is everything just varying shades of grey with you?"

She rolls her eyes. "You know what? This is good. We now know this won't work—in any way, shape, or form."

I rake my fingers through my hair. "That's what I've been trying to say."

"Okay. Experiment failed. We can move on." Em pauses, her face softening. "For what it's worth, you seem like a pretty okay guy."

I can feel my scowl softening. "You're pretty okay yourself."

She gives me a small smile. The tug I feel inside me when her face lights up makes me wonder for the millionth time if I'm doing the right thing by letting her go. But I have to. If not for me, I need to do the right thing for her.

An awkward silence swells between us like a canyon, the divide growing larger by the second. "All right," Em says, taking a step back. "I need to go."

I raise my needle-nose pliers. "Me, too."

She pauses, licking her lips. "You can still come by for coffee. I promise not to spit in all of your drinks…just a couple."

I almost laugh. Then I hear a man's voice booming from the next aisle over. Invisible fingers curl around my throat threatening to choke me. I'd recognize that voice anywhere.

"Don't get so freaked out." Emily frowns. "I was just kidding about the spitting. I swear I wouldn't do that."

I crouch low, pressing a finger to my lips.

Placing a hand on her hip, Emily arches an eyebrow. "What the hell are you doing? Are you having another attack?"

"No," I practically spit. "It's my dad." I point at the next aisle over.

"So?"

"*So,* I've successfully avoided him for several years, and I'm not about to stop now," I answer, keeping my voice low.

She ducks her head, peering through the shelves. "Why?"

I give her a look. "That answer would require more time than I have right now."

"And you called *me* a coward."

"You really want to play the hypocrite game right now? What would you do if it was *your mother* in the next aisle?"

Biting her lip, she glances over her shoulder at the

sound of the approaching voice. "You're right." She gives my shoulder a gentle push. "Get the hell out of here."

I make a face and gesture to my cane. "Stealth and speed aren't things I have anymore."

"I *know*." She gives me another push. "That's why I'm going to stall your dad so you can get out of here."

"How are you—"

"Don't worry about it," she says, shoving me again. "Just get the hell out of here."

Before she can push me again, I spot the polished tip of my father's loafer coming around the corner. I quickly spin on my heels and hobble down the aisle as fast as my damn knee will let me.

"Hi," Emily calls out behind me. "You look like a man of impeccable taste."

"I, uh, excuse me?" my father responds.

"I'm redoing my apartment, and I can't decide between these two shades of green. What do you think? Though, now that I'm looking at your tie, I'm wondering if lavender is a better choice."

"I'm sorry?"

"Oh," Em answers, "is your wife the one who makes the decorating decisions? Is that who you're talking to on the phone? Can I speak with her?"

"You want to talk to my wife?"

"Sure," Em answers. "Unless, say, do you have an interior decorator? Ooh! Definitely call them instead. But finish your phone call first. I'll wait."

Discarding my unpurchased pliers in a nearby bin, I almost feel sorry for my dad as I exit through the automatic doors. Then I remember the way he looked at me when I told him I'd enlisted. The fuchsia fury that blazed across his skin and the way the veins pulsed in his temples are still imprinted in my memory.

The screaming that followed, the disappointment and the financial cut-off, none of that bothered me. I expected it. I didn't expect, however, their absence at the airport when I was rolled off the plane in a wheelchair. Or the hours I spent watching luggage spin around and around the carousel as I waited, until the realization finally hit me.

They weren't coming.

That cut deeper than any words ever did.

I climb onto my bike and fasten my cane to the side. After revving the engine, I prepare to leave, but something holds me back.

All these years later, I still remember what it felt like to be abandoned. And I'll be damned if I do it to anyone else.

Muttering a curse under my breath, I know I can't leave her—especially after she just saved my ass. But more than that, I don't want to leave without her. And I'm not going to.

Em exits the store several minutes later. I pull my bike in front of her, blocking her path.

Her eyes widen, a ghost of a grin playing on her lips. "I thought you'd be long gone by now."

"Get on." I motion to the empty spot behind me.

She folds her arms. "I'm borrowing my brother's car. It's right over there."

"And my bike is right here. Get on."

"You literally just told me you don't want a relationship and you don't want a hookup."

I shake my head. "I don't."

"Then what the hell will I be getting myself into if I go home with you?"

"I have no fucking clue." And it's true. I know taking her back with me will mean letting her into my head again, and this time I might not be able to get her out. But the alternative, letting her walk out of my life for good, is no longer an option.

I hold out my hand. "Get on the bike, and let's find out."

Chapter Seventeen

EMILY

I'm an idiot. I'm an idiot. I'm an idiot.

The words echo through my head in a never-ending loop. Even the wind roaring through my ears as we race through the streets on Reece's bike isn't enough to drown out my self-loathing. *God, why?* Why *am I such an idiot?*

I've been with bad-news guys before. I've always been able to leave them on the curb without a twinge of remorse. So what the hell is it about J.Crew that has me coming back for a second serving of heartache?

Not that I'd ever openly admit to letting him hurt me the first time.

But he did.

And what's to stop him from doing it again?

The wind carries a chill that bites into my skin. Before we took off, Reece handed me his jacket and helmet. I nestle deeper into that jacket now, soaking in the spicy scent of Reece's lingering cologne.

A wicked plan crosses my mind. I could steal the jacket. Then I could cuddle inside it whenever I want. Even as I have the thought, however, I know I could never do it. For as much as I like wearing Reece's jacket, I have to admit, I like watching him wear it even more.

Oh my God, I'm so pathetic.

Reece leans into a turn, and I tighten my grip around his waist. I press tighter than I have to, just so I can feel the warmth of him beneath his shirt. It wasn't so long ago that same heat bled into me.

He's using you, the voice whispers. *He's just going to screw you again, only to disappear.*

The thought is sobering, and any warmth I felt quickly fades. It shouldn't bother me. I've used guys dozens of times, and they've used me. So why does the thought of never seeing Reece again squeeze my heart so tightly?

That's ridiculous, I think, shaking my head, trying to loosen the thoughts piling inside. Emily Garrett does not let guys get to her like this. It must be because he's so different from my usual type—the deadbeats, artists, and musicians— that's what makes him so interesting.

I could easily find myself another J.Crew to keep me entertained.

Maybe even a better one.

It's the same sort of lovely lie my brain constructs to keep me drinking. *You haven't had that much. You're still in control.*

Reece pulls into the driveway of a small house—exactly the kind of place I pictured him living in. It's a beige vinyl-sided ranch, with a neat lawn and fenced-in backyard. The landscaping is tidy, not a rock out of place, and the bushes trimmed in symmetrical rectangles.

When he cuts the engine, my heart does a somersault. *Holy shit, I'm actually nervous.* The feeling is quickly squashed by a wave of annoyance. This guy makes me stupid, and I don't like it.

"This is it, in all its glory." After Reece unfastens his cane, he extends a hand to me, helping me off the bike.

I don't know why he says it like that—like it's something to be ashamed of. Sure it's small and boring, but it's a house, with a grownup mortgage and everything. I bet he even has homeowners' insurance.

Once again, I question what the hell I'm doing here. After all, what he said about me in the hardware store was right. I am a fucking coward. Because as much as I want to admit I'm an adult, all of this stuff—houses with mortgages, insurance, 401Ks, the potential for whatever Reece and I have between us—scares the shit out of me.

Reece escorts me inside, which is just as tidy and boring as the outside. Except for a folded American flag encased in glass and a box displaying several mounted military medals, the house contains no distinctive touches. Bare gray walls, beige couch, and a flat screen television are all that make up his living room. The only item with any personality is the slightly askew tackle box on the glass coffee table.

"You don't like it."

Startled, I turn to find him grinning.

"It's nice…for a serial killer."

He laughs. "Please, don't hold back."

"Never do." I shrug out of his jacket and toss it on the nearby recliner. He doesn't say anything, but his face twitches slightly.

A neatness freak, huh? Deciding to have a little fun, I flop down on the couch and put my feet on the coffee table.

He stiffens.

"If I put a piece of coal between your ass cheeks right now, would I get a diamond?" I ask.

His eyes narrow. "Hilarious." He motions to the kitchen. "You want a beer? I could use a beer."

I make a face. "I always want a beer, remember?"

"Oh, shit, that's right. I'm sorry."

I wave a hand in the air. "That doesn't mean you can't have one."

"No." He settles into the arm chair across from me. "I'm good."

A heavy silence settles over us, making me squirm. "So what the hell are we doing, exactly?"

He sighs, combing his fingers through his hair. "I was hoping you knew."

This makes me laugh. "Nope. Not a fucking clue."

He nods but stays silent.

"Well then." I stand, brushing off my jeans. "The awkward encounter, followed by the bike ride, followed by more awkward silence has been fun. But now I'm going to get an Uber back to my car."

"No."

I tilt my head. "No?"

His eyes meet mine. It's the first time I notice he's got the face of an angel but the eyes of a devil. "Stay." He pauses. "Please."

I slowly lower myself back to the couch. I hate the power he has over me, but at the same time it gives me a rush. "What the hell do you want from me, Reece?"

"I don't know. Do you?"

I thought I did. I thought I was only after fun, until our night together. That was before he got inside my head. It wasn't fun after that. "I'm going to be totally honest. It hurt when you stopped coming around."

His jaw tightens. "That wasn't my intention. I thought I was doing you a favor."

"I don't need you to take care of me."

"Em, you don't understand how fucked up I am. You have no idea what you'd be getting into with me."

He drops his head into his hands and sinks into a chair, looking very much broken. Seeing him this way pulls at my heart. I make my way to him, stopping when my knees bump his.

He looks up, lines of confusion wrinkling his brow. "What—"

"I might not know what I'm getting myself into," I say, settling onto his lap and twining my fingers around his neck, "but don't I deserve the chance to decide for myself if you're worth it or not?"

"I'm not," he says flatly.

"Again, you don't get to decide that for me."

"I don't have the strength to keep pushing you away." He traces the ink down my arms. A delicious trail of shivers follow his touch. I arch my back and his eyes darken with hunger. "The war didn't destroy me. But you, Emily Garrett, you just might."

I kiss him, urgently, desperate to swallow his words as well as my own. Because the truth is, given my rapidly crumbling walls, he could just as easily do the same to me.

Chapter Eighteen

Despite his injured knee, he's able to stand and pick me up.

I gasp. "Reece. You could hurt yourself. Put me down."

"I'll pay for it tomorrow. But right now it's worth it."

I hook my arms around his neck as he carries me, hobbling the entire way, to the bedroom. He gently sets me down on the bed and stands.

"I want to do things differently tonight."

I tilt my head. "What do you mean?"

He sits down next to me and slowly pulls his shirt over his head. Just looking at the tight muscles of his chest fills me with desire. "I want to take things slow."

I try not to let my disappointment show. "You know I like it rough. You won't hurt me."

"I know." He cups my face with his hand before sliding it down my neck. Sparks ignite a trail beneath his fingers, and I shiver. "But I think *I* used to like it this way—*before*. I can't remember. And I want to."

His admission stabs my heart, and I nod. "Whatever you want."

"You."

"I'm yours, baby." Licking my lips, I ask, "What would you like me to do first?"

He pauses, considering for a moment. "Undress for me."

"You got it." I grasp the hem of my shirt and pull it over my head. Thank God I grabbed my lacy red pushup bra today instead of my dingy boring racerback. Pushing up onto my knees, I unbutton my jeans, shimmy out of them, and toss them beside the bed.

"Undress *all* the way."

I smile. I guess it wouldn't have mattered if I wore the ugly bra, considering how long he would have seen me in it. Taking my time, I unhook the back and slide each strap, one at a time, down my arms. I let it fall to the floor. Next, I hook my thumbs under the lacy edge of my panties and slide them down, one slow inch at a time.

Reece grins and his eyes darken with hunger. I'm no stranger to guys looking at me with lust, but this is something else. He said he wanted to do things differently tonight, but he has the same look in his eye he had the night we first had sex. Dangerous. Like he's all but ready to devour me. He hasn't even touched me and already my breath comes in quick gasps.

"Now undress me."

I climb off the bed and kneel in front of him. Maybe this is going to be more fun than I thought. He's already straining against his jeans when I pop open the button. I make sure to run my hand over him as I pull the zipper down.

Reece's head rolls back and he lets out a moan.

That's all the invitation I need. I slip my hand under the band of his boxer briefs and ensnare his shaft. The skin is so velvety and soft to the touch. He pulses with need as I glide my fingers from shaft to tip and back again.

He lets out a low growl that rumbles deep from within his chest. I can't help but grin. I love making him want me. Desperately. Completely.

Leaning forward, I lick the tip of his dick.

Reece sucks in a breath.

Before he can exhale, I part my lips and take him into my mouth as deep as I dare.

He leans back. *"Oh, fuck,"* he mutters, which only makes me smile.

I glide my tongue around the thickness of him as I work my way up and down. Up and down.

Like before, he winds his fingers into my hair. But this time, instead of tightening them into fists, his hold is gentle.

"God, Em. Oh God."

I wind my way, up and down. Up and down. Spiraling my tongue as I work, until finally, he pushes me away with a sharp intake of breath. "I don't want to. Not yet."

"Really? I don't mind. I actually like—"

"Not tonight." He reaches for my hand, and I give it to him. He helps me to my feet and guides me down onto the bed.

He stands over me for several moments, his eyes taking in every inch of my body until I squirm under the weight of his gaze.

"What are you doing?"

"You're so beautiful."

I roll my eyes. "Reece, you're already going to get laid tonight. You don't have to feed me lines."

"No lines." He climbs onto the bed and straddles me. "Just the truth." His eyes blaze with a dark hunger that sets every nerve in my body aflame. He wants me. *Me.* And it's that look in his eyes—like I'm something to be desired—that makes me feel more beautiful than his words ever did.

He starts slow, running his fingers along my waist, up my

arms, and to my hands. I shiver beneath his touch, as a need builds between my legs. Reflexively, my hips buck forward.

Reece answers by placing his palm on me, pressing down on the hidden sweet spot just beneath my pelvic bone.

I gasp as the strings of pleasure immediately tighten inside me. He grinds his palm against me in a slow, smooth rhythm. Syrupy sweet ecstasy followed by just enough of a pause that I can remember how to breathe.

He continues to caress me, making me tighten with pleasure. The pressure inside me builds with each glide of his skin. Hot, melted sugar. Over and over. Building to the point of painful need as I writhe against him. And still, it's not enough. I want more. I want *him.*

"Please, Reece," I pant. "Please. I want you."

"If that's what you want."

"Yes. God, yes." He takes his hand away and, even though he didn't push me over the edge, the throbbing he leaves behind lets me know I'm dangerously close.

Reece slides his jeans off and tosses them aside. While I struggle to even out my breathing, he opens his nightstand, shuffles inside, and withdraws a condom.

"Can I?" I grab it from him before he can answer. I'm just desperate to touch him again. After sliding the condom on his dick, I get a couple good rubs in before he catches my wrists, a devilish grin on his lips.

"Bad girl."

I shrug. No point denying the truth.

Still holding onto my wrists, he raises my arms above my head and settles between my legs. The moment the head of his penis touches me I tighten with a need so great, I ache.

Rotating his hips, he grazes my outer folds. I whimper and thrust my hips toward him. "Please. Just take me already."

Chuckling, he stops moving. "I love it when you beg."

I open my mouth to reply when his lips crash into mine.

His kiss is a hungry storm, a force so strong, I'm overpowered in an instant. His tongue strikes with the heat of lightening, leaving me trembling.

He moves from my mouth to the sensitive skin just below my ear. I gasp as his tongue traces a trail down my neck, along my collar bone, and between my breasts. He traces each nipple with his tongue, and they tighten harder with each pass.

When he takes one between his teeth, I cry out. He creates a rhythm of tongue and teeth. Pleasure and pain. The switch is both dizzying and electrifying.

He shifts his hips, and suddenly he's inside me. I cry out, from the pleasure of having him, at long last, inside me, unwinding the coiled muscles so tight with need for him.

Lacing his fingers through mine, he keeps my hands above my head as he thrusts. The pressure low inside begins to build, filling me with warm honey with each grind of his hips. More and more until it overflows.

I scream as shockwave after shockwave crashes through me. I buck and writhe against him, hooking my legs around his waist to keep the waves of pleasure from carrying me away.

Reece groans, and his fingers tighten on mine. His grinding becomes erratic, until he pushes into me one last time. I can feel his dick pulse inside me as he comes.

I melt beneath him. No bones. Liquid muscle. Basically human pudding.

Slowly, he untangles our fingers, slides an arm around my neck, and drops onto the bed beside me.

I keep my legs wrapped around his waist. I'm not ready to let go.

"That was amazing." His voice is thick with satisfaction and fatigue.

"Amazing," I agree, resting my head on his chest.

I listen to the soft thump of his heart until his breathing evens out and I know he's asleep.

And for once, I have no desire to sneak out of bed, get dressed, and run back home. With his arm around my shoulders, and our hearts echoing each other's beats, I'm happy exactly where I am.

Amazing.

Chapter Nineteen

Emily

"Em, wake up." A hand brushes the hair off my face.

I blink several times, pulling myself from dreamless sleep. The details come slowly. The bed is too soft, the sheets smell like lavender, and there is a distinct absence of warm man beside me. "Reece? Is everything okay?"

"I want to take you somewhere. If you hurry, we can get something to eat on the way."

I rub the heels of my hands against my eyes to clear up the darkness. When that doesn't help, I realize the darkness won't leave because it *is* dark. I turn to the nightstand. A digital clock reads three thirty in the morning.

I sink back into the pillow. "Reece, go back to bed. You're sleepwalking or something."

He chuckles. "I'm wide awake. Come on. We want to beat the sun."

"Said no sane person ever." I throw an arm over my face.

"Come on, Sleeping Beauty." He snatches my wrist and

pulls me into an upright position while I groan. "We have to leave now so we can stop by your apartment. You need to change."

"Change? For what? My incarceration? Because I swear, if you drag me out of this bed before the sun comes up, I will end you, Reece."

"Challenge accepted." Before I can react, he yanks the covers off of me.

With a gasp, I clutch a pillow to my now freezing body.

He leans against the doorway, watching me, with a big stupid grin on his face. "Oh good, you're up. Now hurry." He claps his hands together before spinning around and leaving me alone.

Confused—and even more pissed—I scramble for my clothes. When I'm dressed, he meets me at the door with fishing rods and a tackle box.

"Seriously?" I ask. "You're taking me fishing? Don't you have school or something?"

"I'm calling in sick today."

"To go fishing."

"Have you ever been?"

"Once." I nod. "My dad took me before he died. He bought me a pink Barbie fishing rod. I think I was like five or something?"

"You still have the rod?"

"Are you kidding? It's long gone."

"That's too bad."

I shrug. "That's life."

He doesn't move for several heartbeats. When he does, he limps over to me and kisses the top of my head. The gesture is so tender, so foreign to me, it makes me inhale sharply.

I could easily stay this way all day, wrapped in his arms. At the same time, that feeling of want is so strange, I grow uncomfortable. "We should get going." My voice trembles slightly as I wriggle out of his grip.

"You're right," he says but doesn't move. Instead, he watches me, his eyes searching for — I'm not sure what exactly. I squirm under the weight of his gaze. "We should hurry."

He drops me off at my apartment so I can change into "something I'm not afraid to get dirty." He's back at my door twenty minutes later, holding a brand new pink Barbie fishing pole.

"What the hell is that?" I ask, laughing.

He grins that rare, lopsided grin of his. "For you. Seemed important."

"Yeah, when I was five."

"If you don't like it, how come you're smiling?" He takes me by the hand and leads me outside to his waiting bike. His own disassembled poles as well as his tackle box are tucked inside his saddlebag.

"You're so stupid," I tell him, holding the rod close as I climb on behind him. "The fish are going to make fun of me."

"They wouldn't dare make fun of my girl," he answers, starting the bike. "I'd kick their fish asses."

My girl. A secret thrill jolts through my body at his words. Just as quickly, I give myself a mental kick for reacting like a schoolgirl. What is it about him that makes me so giddy?

It's so early the streets are practically deserted. It doesn't take long before we're out of the city. Thirty minutes later, Reece turns onto a dirt-patched gravel road. After several feet, he stops the bike and kills the engine. He looks at me over his shoulder. "We walk from here."

We dismount. He retrieves his poles and tackle from the saddlebag, while I continue to clutch my ridiculous baby fishing pole. The sun is considering its ascent, not quite rising, but purpling the edges of the black sky. "This way." He nods toward a line of shadowed trees several yards away.

"I can't believe I'm in the middle of nowhere, at this

ungodly hour, with a pink fishing pole," I mutter.

Reece smirks. "It's great, isn't it? Let's hurry." After unhooking his cane, he trudges down the road. I can't help noticing how light his steps have become, despite the uneven terrain.

The road narrows the farther we walk, becoming little more than a dirt strip beyond the trees. We follow it as it winds through the tall grass and down a small slope. It stops at the muddy edge of a lake. The glittering water reflects the disappearing moon in the lavender sky.

The beauty of it makes me pause.

"I told you it was great, didn't I?" Reece tugs the belt loop on my jeans, pulling me toward him.

I nod. "It's amazing."

"A buddy of mine's dad owns this property. We've been fishing on it since we were kids." He lets go of my belt loop and rests his hand on the small of my back. If it was any other guy, I'd want to shy away from the touch. But not with Reece. I want to lean into him and close the distance between us.

I also don't want to ruin it. This whole being-around-a-guy-because-I-actually-like-him thing is new to me, and I still haven't figured out the rules. "I never would have pegged you as someone who fished," I tell him.

He arches an eyebrow. "Why's that?"

"A J.Crew guy like yourself? Shouldn't you be playing golf or polo or something?"

"Polo?" He laughs. "Nah. I only do that on the weekend."

The sound of his laugh coats my insides like warm honey. I elbow him in the ribs, which only makes him chuckle harder. "But seriously," I say, "why fishing?"

He's quiet so long I think he's not going to answer. But then he says, "It's the only thing I have left that the war didn't change or take away. Fishing, for me, is exactly the same as it was before I went to the desert. Nothing else is like that."

I say nothing.

He points to a patch of tall grass by the water. "That's the magic spot. We'll set up there."

Following him, I watch as he runs the line through his poles. Then he helps me do the same to my pole. He doesn't make fun of me, even when I string it through the wrong loop twice.

When I finally do get it right, he helps me add a bobber and hook then gives me a ten-minute lecture on the pros and cons of all the little, wiggly, rubber things in his tackle box. I immediately forget everything he said. Despite smelling terrible, the wiggly, rubber things are colorful and glittery. So, at the very least, I learn fish have good taste.

After baiting our hooks, we cast our lines into the lake and sit on a nearby log.

"Now what?" I ask.

Reece stretches his legs in front of him. "We wait for the magic to happen."

As far as I'm concerned, the magic's already happening. The sun peeks over the horizon, an orange halo that sets the lake on fire. I can't help but gasp. "It's beautiful."

"Beautiful," Reece agrees.

I turn to find it's not the sunset he's watching, but me.

My cheeks burn, and I look away.

"Thank you," he says.

"For?"

"Coming here. With me."

I laugh. "Did I have a choice?"

"Always. And you chose me."

I don't know what to say to that, so I stay silent.

He slowly tightens the line on his fishing rod. "It makes me feel human again."

"What?"

"Your earlier question," he answers, keeping his eyes on

the lake. "Why fishing? War takes so much of your humanity away. I forget sometimes, what it means to be human. Fishing reminds me." He meets my eyes. "*You* remind me, too."

Never in my life have I had a man emotionally expose himself in this way. Never have I wanted one to. Until now. Reece's words work their way through my skin and tattoo themselves on my heart. And I'm glad, because I want to keep them with me forever, in a place no one can get to.

Reece's bobber twitches, and he straightens. When nothing more happens, his shoulders relax. "I want to know more about you. Why all the tattoos?"

I glance at the artwork decorating both arms and smile. "My brother did them. He's an amazing artist who owns his own studio. Of course he didn't want to do it, because I'm his baby sister who needs coddling. But when I turned eighteen, I threatened to go get my ink done at a crappy place, so he agreed."

I run my finger down the images woven together in swirls of color. "Each image represents something special to me." I pull down the collar of my shirt, exposing the police badge over my heart. "This one is for Daddy." I tap the star on my left wrist. "This one is, too. He always called me his little star." I twist to show him the cupcake on my right bicep. "This is for Grandma. Cupcakes were the first things she taught me to bake."

"They're amazing," he says.

I shake my head. "Grandma gets the credit. I just follow her recipes."

"That's crap," he says. "Baking is more than following recipes. It requires talent. Take my sister for example. She can't boil an egg to save her life. I, on the other hand, can make a beef wellington that will melt in your mouth."

"You can cook?"

He shrugs. "Just another of my many skills."

I chuckle, and he smiles in return.

"Seriously, though, you have real talent. You should do something with it."

I roll my eyes. "Like what?"

"I don't know." He's silent for a moment as he adjusts his fishing line. "That coffee shop you work for? Their Danishes and coffee cake suck. What if you made them instead?"

I make a face. "I don't know. My boss gets that stuff at the local warehouse store, and she's pretty set in her ways."

"If she tastes your food, there's no way she won't change her mind. People will be breaking down the doors for it."

"Shut up." Smiling, I bump his shoulder with mine.

"Is it something you enjoy doing?" he asks.

"I love it," I answer, surprising myself with how quickly the answer falls off my tongue.

"Then it's worth pursuing."

"Huh. Maybe." I say this even as my mind races with excitement. Still, I know better than to get my hopes up. What if Reece is exaggerating how good my baked goods are? What if everyone else hates them? Am I really ready to face that type of failure?

He places his hand on my wrist, and I realize I've been strumming my fingers on my knee. He gives me a reassuring squeeze. "Everything's going to be okay."

I make a face. "How do you know?"

"Oh, I don't." He stretches his arms over his head. "But at least we have each other."

"And what are *we* exactly?" I ask, smirking.

"Together." He leans over to kiss the top of my head. A flurry of butterflies swirls inside my stomach. "That's good enough, right?"

I rest my head on his shoulder. "Yup," I agree. "That's good enough."

Chapter Twenty

REECE

"Selfie!" Em squeals, shoving her phone into my hand before hooking her arm around my neck. With her other hand, she holds up the bluegill she reeled in.

I try not to laugh as I position her phone. I can't remember when I smiled so much. Something about her giggle makes me forget myself, every time. "Are you sure you want to take a picture of that pathetic minnow? It's embarrassing."

"It's my first fish," she answers, jabbing me in the chest with her index finger. "I'm documenting this historic occasion before I release him. It's a shame I didn't bring a barbell with me. Then we could be twins." She points to the piercing above her lip. "He'd be the most bad ass blue gill ever."

After I snap the photo, Em hands me her pole and snatches her phone. "Oh yeah," she says, scrolling through the photos. "That's definitely a keeper. You want me to send it to you?"

"Absolutely."

Smiling, she types furiously. A moment later my phone buzzes in my pocket.

Grinning, she says, "I'm going to send it to Ash, too. I want her to know I've found my true calling. Master of the Barbie pole." She pauses, tilting her head. "That would be a really fucked up strip club." Before I can respond, she resumes typing. "You care if I post it on Instagram?"

I hesitate a fraction of a second before answering. "No."

Emily must have sensed my reluctance because her smile wilts. "It's not a big deal. I don't have to or anything."

Damn it, Reece. Way to go and screw things up again.

"It's not what you think," I tell her.

She turns away. "You don't have to explain yourself to me."

I grab her wrists before she shuts me out entirely. "Listen, I'm still stuck in military mode. And before...before everything went to shit, we weren't allowed to post anything about ourselves online. But that's different now. I'm out, even though I don't think I'll ever feel entirely free."

Her face slowly softens. "I'm sorry. I didn't realize."

I draw her closer to me. "You have nothing to be sorry for. These are my demons. My war."

I watch her struggle for words, chewing them thoroughly before asking, "What did you do exactly?"

This is the point I usually turn away or say I'm not ready to talk about it. But not this time. I owe Em at least this. "I was in One Sixtieth SOAR. Otherwise known as a Night Stalker."

"Whoa," she whispers. "That sounds intense."

"Death waits in the dark," I mutter, staring out at the water.

"What?"

I shake my head. "Nothing. Just our motto."

Her eyes widen with horror. "You had to kill people?"

I can't help it, I laugh. "Em, it's war."

"But what I mean is you, yourself, killed people."

This time I don't laugh. "Em, it's war."

"Jesus," she mutters. "No wonder you're fucked up."

I nod as I unhook her fish and place it back in the water. It kicks its tail in indignation before swimming away. "Killing the enemy doesn't fuck you up as much as watching them kill your brothers."

She waits, not saying a word, not asking or pressing forward. The bullet around my neck grows heavy, as if encouraging me to go on. Maybe it's finally time to do just that.

"Chad."

She blinks.

"He loved motorcycles, the Razorbacks, and he wouldn't shut up about going to school to become a veterinarian. He had a fiancée back home in Mississippi. Sherill, or Sherry, or something. They were going to have a summer wedding. She wanted him to wear a pink tie and cummerbund." I chuckle, remember Chad's disgust at this.

Emily presses a hand to her mouth, horror filling her eyes.

"Our Little Bird was shot down. I don't know how long I was unconscious. When I came to, there was so much blood. My knee was destroyed—I couldn't walk. Until I heard Chad scream. I practically dragged myself the entire way. In the end, it didn't matter. I was too late."

The words I've been so afraid to speak for so long come to life before me. Suddenly I'm back in the hellish wasteland of the desert. The smoke and gasoline from the flame-engulfed helicopter burns my nostrils. Jason—we called him Cheetah, because he was some big track star back home—hangs out the busted windshield. He doesn't move as the flames eat away his flesh.

For a moment, horror paralyzes me. Then I hear the scream, and I'm propelled forward, through the smoke, through the pain, through the blood.

Gun in hands, I crawl on my belly until I crest the hill. He's on his knees. The enemy has his filthy fingers curled in Chad's hair, pulling his head back. With his other hand he brings a large blade to Chad's neck.

One heartbeat.

Not enough time to scream. Aim. Or pull a trigger.

But enough time to die.

The enemy slices the knife across Chad's neck.

My pulse thunders inside my head, drowning out all sound. I don't remember screaming, but I must have, because the enemy releases Chad's head and pulls a gun, aiming it at me. Even though my gun is in my hands, my blood-soaked fingers fumble on the trigger.

Even from a distance, I can see the rise in the enemy's chest, a sure sign he's preparing to fire.

This is it. The moment I've waited for. *I would rather die than quit.* The Night Stalker motto plays through my head. But they're not just words. *I would rather die than quit.* It's the truth in my blood, reaffirmed with each beat of my heart.

The end. My end.

With as much energy as I can muster, I position my gun on the dune and take aim. If I'm going to die, I'm going to die fighting.

But Chad has other ideas. Even with the gap in his throat and a steady ribbon of blood pouring down his neck, he rears his head back, smashing the enemy's groin. The enemy cries out, doubling over.

Chad's garbled cry is thick with blood.

The enemy, still on the ground, places the barrel of his gun to Chad's temple.

My finger moves, instinct and years of training guiding it. I pull the trigger twice.

Several shots ring out, nearly simultaneously. I don't

know whose was first, mine or the enemy's. Sand spurts from the ground where the enemy's bullets land. I don't wait to see if mine hit or not.

Chad is gone. Jason is gone. The others I'm sure are gone, too. They've all left me alone in this desert hell. If the enemy is still alive, at least he can reunite me with the others.

Dragging myself to my feet, I run. The pain in my leg is so intense my vision goes fuzzy around the edges. I'm seconds from passing out, so I push myself harder, faster.

When I get to Chad, the smell of blood is so thick it stings my nostrils. His uniform is soaked with it, making it appear black in the twilight.

"You goddamned asshole," I scream, grabbing the front of his shirt with my fists and shaking him. Blood still runs from the wound in his neck and temple. His helmet rolls off his head. Bits of bone, brain, and other things are splattered inside. Along with something shiny. A bullet. I grab it without thinking.

"You mother fucker," I yell. He's gone, but maybe there's a part of him still lingering nearby, a part that can still hear me.

"This was my fucking bullet." I pull his body up only to slam it back to the sand. Over and over. "My bullet and you stole it from me."

The enemy is slumped beside him. It's obvious he's gone, too. But there's no way I'm going to let him travel into the unknown with Chad. Screaming, I fire into what's left of his skull, over and over, spraying chunks and bits all over the sand. Maybe if I shoot him enough, I can make him disappear entirely. Too bad I run out of ammo before I can find out.

Chest still heaving, and unconsciousness wrapping around me like a warm blanket, I slump to the ground beside the empty corpses. My eyelids grow heavy. I know if I let them fall, I won't be able to open them again.

Part of me hopes I never do.

When I open my eyes again, the twilight has given way to the soft pink and orange lines of morning. The smell of blood fades, as does the pain in my legs. Slowly, I come to realize I'm not in the desert but sitting on a log beside a lake.

My fingers ache, and I realize my hold on the fishing rod is vise-tight. Thread by thread my muscles unwind, until I slump against the log.

Gone. The desert. The blood. Chad. It's all gone.

"Reece?"

I jerk back, startled to find I'm not alone. I'm always alone. Except now. Emily sits beside me, an emotionless mask on her face. How much did I tell her before the desert stole me back?

"The bullet." She reaches out tentatively and touches the cold metal beneath my shirt. I flinch. "That's *your* bullet, isn't it?"

Shit. I said too much. I turn, staring out at the lake, letting the silence be my answer.

Her fingers slide down my shirt before dropping to her side. An ache fills me at the lack of her touch, and I fight to keep from reaching out to her.

"I can give you what you need," she says. "Time, space, comfort, silence. Whatever you need."

"Doesn't matter what you can give me, Em. That's the problem. You'll give, and you'll give, and you'll give till you can't give anymore. And it won't be enough. I'm broken. Haunted by nightmares when I'm asleep and awake. I have nothing to give you in return."

"That's bullshit." She scoots closer to me.

Without thinking, I bring my arm around her shoulders and pull her close. Immediately the shadow of the ever-encroaching desert recedes. It's as if Emily is an anchor, somehow tethering me to this reality. "Really? What can I give you?"

She looks thoughtful. "Whatever it is, I think you already have."

I tilt my head. "Care to explain?"

She shrugs. "I don't know that I can. It's more a feeling. You make me feel better about myself. That I'm more than a loser party girl."

I take her chin in my hand, forcing her to look at me. "You are *not* a loser. You are amazing."

She laughs. "See? That's what I'm talking about."

"Em, I'm serious. Not knowing what you want out of life doesn't make you a bad person. I think you'll figure things out at the right time."

"I hope you're right."

"Sometimes that's enough."

"What?"

"Hope." I drop my hand, releasing her.

"Do you have hope?" she asks.

"I do now." I set my rod aside, lean forward, and kiss her. We've kissed before, but this time, it's different. Every kiss with Emily has tasted of hunger. This one aches, hard, fast, and desperate. I realize, as she's nestled in my arms, she's the first good thing that's happened to me since the desert. And if I'm not careful, she could slip away like every other good thing in my life has.

At the thought, I pull her tighter, hoping to keep her from fading out of my grip.

As if she can read my mind, she pulls back with a gasp. "Reece. I'm here. Don't worry. I'm here."

I rest my forehead against hers, needing proof. Needing her heat, her touch, her breath. She's here. Yes.

But for how long?

Chapter Twenty-One

EMILY

Never in a million years would I have imagined myself in a relationship, let alone loving it.

It's been over a month since Reece and I surrendered to whatever the hell this is between us. We've never tried to define or label whatever *it* is. Maybe that's for the best. It's this burrito of good, comfort, and reliability all wrapped up in a steamy tortilla of hot bedroom action.

What's an even bigger surprise is how much I'm loving it. Me, the girl who never wanted to be tied down, is now craving all the little relationship moments I've been scared of for so long.

I love seeing him at the coffee shop every morning. I'll hand him his Americano (extra hot, like him), which will already be made and waiting. He'll give me a kiss, and I'll adjust his crooked tie before he darts out the door on his way to school.

I love having dinner together nearly every weeknight. And, if he doesn't have too many papers to grade, I know we'll end up tangled in the sheets afterward. And if, for whatever reason, we can't get together, I know I'll get a phone call or a text from him, telling me he's missing me and wishing me goodnight.

Last Saturday we saw a movie with Ash and Lane. My brother, for the first time ever, didn't threaten to kill the guy I was with. They even bonded over cars or motorcycles or some shit. I'm not exactly sure, as the conversation was too boring to follow.

I like the coffee mixed with morning kisses. I like the weekend bike rides down country roads, and I like having him on my couch, right this second, with his shoes kicked off and a stack of papers on his lap. His forehead is creased in lines of concentration. I quickly snap a picture of him, before tucking my phone in my pocket and resuming my cookie icing.

When I'm finished, I cup a still warm cookie in my hand, walk it over to him, and wave it in front of his nose.

He groans, dropping the tests on his lap, along with his red pen. "No, Em, not again." He pushes the cookie away.

I stick out my bottom lip in a pout. "I thought you loved my sugar cookies."

"I do." He pulls off his glasses. "That's the problem. I've gained nearly fifteen pounds, thanks to you. I can't do it anymore. We need real food."

"Cookies *are* real food."

He snorts. "You know what I mean. Let's go out."

I roll my eyes as I bite into the cookie. "You don't like to go out."

"I'm having a good day today," he argues. "I can handle it. Especially if we go somewhere quiet." He arches a delicious eyebrow. "Dimly lit."

"Ooh, okay." I plop down onto his lap, not caring about the tests beneath me. "What about that Asian fusion place on the west end?"

His smile withers. "What about someplace else?"

"What gives? You love Asian food. That place has amazing sushi."

"I know." He eases the tests out from under me and stacks them neatly.

"And so now we hate restaurants with good food? Why?"

He sighs. "What *gives* is my parents also love that place. If we go there, we might run into them, and that's a chance I don't want to take."

"Why are you scared of your parents? After everything you faced in the desert?"

He makes a face. "I'm not scared of my parents. I just don't want anything to do with them."

"Because," I prompt.

He makes a face. "You're not going to let this go, are you?"

"Nope."

He sighs again. "Fine. My parents are very wealthy, and they've used money my entire life to control me. Play this sport and we'll take you to the toy store. Earn straight A's and we'll buy you whatever video games you want. Get accepted into this college and we'll buy you a sports car. I had a trust fund I was going to use to buy a fishing boat and RV so I could travel the country and fish. My parents took the trust fund away the day I enlisted."

"God, I'm sorry."

He shrugs. "It's just money. Yeah, it sucks, but what really pissed me off is they would punish me just for making my own decisions. I remember watching the news after that marathon bombing, and seeing the face of that four-year-old kid that died. I can't explain it; I just knew I had to do something. I didn't enlist to spite them. I enlisted because I felt a sense of duty. But they didn't care. After my discharge, they never showed at the airport to pick me up. Just another way they punished me for going against them."

"Reece, that's awful."

"It's fine. I made it through the surgeries and physical therapy on my own. Eventually my sister came to visit me. My parents must not have realized I was permanently disabled, because after her visit, the phone calls started. They left so many apologetic messages I had to change my number. I'm done with them."

"So that's why you hid from your dad in the hardware store."

"Exactly."

I wrap my arms around his neck. "My mom is the queen of guilt. We don't have the best relationship, but we still *have* a relationship."

He grunts. "And your point?"

"My *point* is she fought breast cancer several years after my dad died. Even though she makes me insane, I can't imagine how awful it would be if something happened to her and she didn't know I loved her." I give him a pointed look.

"What makes you think I love my parents?"

I shake my head. "I guess I don't know either way. But, God forbid, what if they died tomorrow? Would you be okay leaving things as they are now?"

His jaw hardens and he looks away. "I don't know."

"I'm not saying you have to go back to being their dutiful son, complete with Thanksgivings and Sunday dinners, but maybe you could take one night to hash things out. That way you won't get stuck wondering what might have been."

He's quiet for nearly a minute. Finally, he turns to me with a smirk. "How can someone so sexy be so completely annoying at the same time?"

"It's a gift. So, are you going to make the call?"

"Not so fast." He places his hands on my hips, pulling me against him. "Speaking of your many gifts, let's talk about another one."

"Nah, let's not." It's then I realize the real reason he put his hands on my waist isn't to kick off a sexy-time session—it's to trap me. Damn, sexy, conniving bastard. I try to squirm away, but his hold on me only tightens. "Look, I know you're trying to keep me from running away. But I can't lie. I'm a little turned on."

"Later." He grins devilishly. "We're talking now. It's obvious you have a gift for baking." He wipes away a stray crumb from my lower lip. "Have you brought up the possibility of you selling your baked goods in the coffee shop?"

"Are you sure you don't want to fool around? There's always time to talk later." I wriggle against his lap until he grows hard beneath me.

Reece groans and tips his head back. "Em, you drive me crazy."

"I know." I wrap my arms around his neck.

Slowly, he lifts his head up. He slides his hands beneath my shirt, his fingers gliding up my ribs until they hit the edge of my bra.

I inhale sharply.

"Two can play this game, little girl." His voice has turned husky and it tightens things low inside me.

I lick my lips. "Oh, yes, please. Let's play."

He grabs my wrists from behind his neck and tosses me off of his lap, onto the couch beside him. Just as quickly, he straddles me and pins my arms over my head. "We're going to make a deal," he says. "I'll call my parents and arrange for *one* dinner. In turn, you have to talk to the coffee shop about selling your baked goods. Do we have a deal?" Before I can answer, he dips his head and kisses my lips. Soft brushes of satin broken up with flashes of teeth.

I moan. "You're not playing fair. I'd agree to anything right now."

When he talks, his words are hot against my neck. "That is

a hell of a tempting offer."

My desire is so hot it burns like flames beneath my skin. Even so, a few coherent thoughts manage to pass through my brain. My baking is very personal. If I were rejected in any way, it would feel like my grandma was being rejected along with me. I don't know that I could stand that. "What if my boss hates my baking?" I ask, my words coming out in heavy pants.

"Impossible."

"What if she still says no?"

"What if you never find out?" He kisses up my neck and takes hold of my earlobe between my teeth.

I exhale loudly. "Why is this so important to you?"

"Because you're important to me." He takes a handful of my hair and tilts my head back, forcing me to look at him. "And you're happiest when you're baking."

"I can think of one activity that comes in at a close second."

His fingers tighten in my hair. The flashes of pain quickly melt in heated pleasure.

I gasp as need swells inside me.

"We're not going any further until you agree to talk to your boss."

"Sexual blackmail? Not cool, Reece Montgomery."

He grins. "I fight dirty."

I give a frustrated growl. "I don't need you, you know. I *can* take care of myself."

"Don't doubt it." He grins. "But can you take care of yourself the way *I* can take care of you?"

He has a point.

"Fine. But just so you know, if I agree to your demands, and I talk to my boss, the sex better be damn good."

His hold on me tightens and his eyes flash with that look of dark hunger that makes me pulse with desire. "Oh, you can count on it."

Chapter Twenty-Two

EMILY

Ashlyn places a hand on my bouncing knee to steady it. "It's okay, Em. Everything's going to be okay." She smiles from her seat beside me in the coffee shop.

I try to smile back, but it feels weak even to me, and I'm pretty sure it falls right off my face. "Thanks for being here."

"Of course, though, I'm not sure I'm going to be much help."

"I'm a nervous wreck." I drum my fingers on the tabletop. "Having you here for moral support is all I need. Plus, you were Alice's favorite employee when you worked here. Maybe she won't reject me in front of you."

"Don't say that. You're not going to get rejected." She shakes her head. "I still can't believe you kept your baking a secret from me all this time. Seriously, all of this looks amazing." She gestures to the plates set before us piled with cupcakes, cookies, Danishes, and sliced banana bread.

I shrug. "I didn't mean to keep it a secret. I haven't baked in a really long time. I wasn't even sure I remembered how."

"Obviously you did," she says, picking up a slice of banana bread and popping it into her mouth. She rolls her eyes heavenward and groans. "Oh my God. So good. When did you start doing this?"

"It's funny. I was in the kitchen one night and inspiration took over. It hasn't let go since."

"Huh. Interesting." She smiles wickedly.

"What? Why are you smiling so weird?"

"Inspiration—is that what we're calling Reece now?"

"Oh, shut up," I say, swatting at her. "It's not like that."

She laughs. "So what if it is like that? It's not a bad thing. You seem really happy, Em. And that makes me really happy, too."

Before I can respond, Alice, owner of Live Wire, approaches our table. She unties her apron before plopping down on the chair across from us. "Sorry I'm late." She runs her fingers through her wispy gray bangs. "The new guy's taking a little longer to catch on than I'd hoped."

I look at him just in time to see him burn his fingers on steam from the espresso maker. He lets out a yelp and drops the cream onto the floor.

"Um, should we help him?" Ashlyn asks.

"Absolutely not." Alice removes her wire-rimmed glasses and wipes them off with her crumpled apron. "How else is he going to learn?"

The sound of glass shattering rings out behind us.

"On second thought," Alice says, "we better make this fast." She sets her glasses aside and folds her fingers together. "I've had a chance to sample everything, Emily, and let me start by saying, I'm impressed."

Her words stun me and I inhale sharply.

Beneath the table Ashlyn bumps my leg with her knee.

"But I'm afraid I'm going to have to be blunt," Alice

continues.

There it is. I exhale in a whoosh.

"I love you, Emily," Alice says. "You know that. I was friends with your mother before you were born, so I've known you your entire life."

Each muscle in my body pulls tight, like a rubber band on the verge of breaking. I don't know where this is going, but I know it can't be good.

"You're a good girl, Emily," she says, patting my hand. "But you have a hard time committing to things."

I feel like I've been slapped in the face. "What does that mean?"

Sighing, Alice pinches the bridge of her nose. "Where do I even begin? First you wanted me to host an open mic night. I said sure, but you'd have to run it. You never even put up the fliers."

Heat burns up my cheeks, and I clench my hands into fists beneath the table.

"This is different," Ashlyn cuts in. "You can't deny she has amazing talent."

"The cupcakes are to die for," she agrees. "But how can I be sure you won't lose interest in baking them tomorrow? Remember when I offered to make you assistant manager, but you declined because you couldn't give up your Saturday nights?"

"I was nineteen," I argue.

"And you're twenty-one now," Annie continues. "How do I know you've changed so much in two years? If you became my baked goods supplier, you would have to deliver your pastries before the sun came up. Every day. Can you really commit to that? Remember when you gave me one-day notice before jetting off to Europe with one of those guys of yours? You left me in a real bind then, Em. I can't afford to make that mistake again."

"I, uh…" I stare at the cookies I spent hours carefully icing. Now all I want to do is throw them on the floor and stomp them into crumbs. God, this was a stupid idea. I'm even more stupid for believing for a second it would have worked out.

I stand suddenly, and the metal feet of the chair squeal against the ceramic tile. Everyone in the coffee shop turns to look at me. If only I could dissolve into the ground and no longer occupy useful space with my worthless self. "I'm sorry," I say, pulling plastic containers out of a bag beneath the table. I pack the pastries in them as quickly as my shaking fingers allow. "You're right. This was a terrible idea."

"Emily." Ashlyn reaches for me, but I withdraw my hand before she can grab it.

"It's fine, I'm fine."

"I tell you what," Alice continues, "how about we revisit this conversation in six months? Prove to me you're ready to take on the added responsibility."

"Yeah, sure," I mumble, shoving the boxes of pastries inside the shopping bag. Heat flushes up my neck and my eyes burn. I bite down on the inside of my cheek to keep from crying. *Don't do it,* I tell myself. *Not in front of them. Not in front of anyone.*

I smooth my skirt as I turn back to the table. "Thank you for your time, Alice. I need to go."

"Emily, I didn't mean to upset you. This isn't a permanent no."

I hold up a hand before she can say more. "It's fine. I'm a big girl. You don't have to sugarcoat it for me."

"So, we'll revisit this again in six months?" She stands and ties her apron around her waist.

It feels like a golf ball-sized lump is wedged inside my throat, keeping me from talking. I nod.

"Good." She glances at the new guy, who's fumbling with

the syrups. "Then I better get back to babysitting."

I don't wait for her to leave before I turn for the door. I refuse to fall apart here. I can't. But I don't even make it two steps before Ashlyn grabs my arm.

"Are you okay?" she asks.

I nod, keeping my eyes trained on the door. For the first time in several months, I'm desperate for a drink. The need swells through my veins, pulsing with each thrum of my heart.

"You're not acting okay."

"I'm fine," I manage to choke out, untangling myself from her grasp. How am I going to break this to Reece? He was so excited for me when he left for school this morning. It's bad enough I let myself down. Now I'm going to let him down, too. Loser Emily strikes again.

"Can I go with you? We can hang out, watch movies—"

"Actually," I cut in, "I'd rather be alone right now."

"Oh." She takes a step back. "Maybe later, then?"

"Later," I echo. Lifting my chin, I march out the door. Outside, I dump the entire bag of pastries into the closest trashcan before heading toward my new car. It's a used Honda Fit. While it's cute, it's not the MINI Convertible I loved so much. The MINI Convertible totaled by a drunk idiot because I was stupid enough to give him the keys.

I let my head fall against the steering wheel as tears well in my eyes. God, will I ever stop being an idiot? I don't blame Alice for not giving me a chance. Of course she thinks I'm a loser—because I *am*.

My phone buzzes inside my pocket, startling me. I pull it out and see the text is from Reece.

So proud of you.

Disgusted, I close the screen. He wouldn't be proud if he could see me now and realize what a miserable failure I am.

My phone buzzes again.

Your bravery inspired me. I called my parents. They want

to meet for dinner tonight. Please come. I can't do this without you.

I toss the phone aside. It makes me sick just looking at the words. He's inspired by my bravery? If only he realized there's nothing here but failure. And when he does realize it, what will he think of me then?

I start my car, undecided where to go. I'm not sure I can face my failure alone, in an empty apartment. At the same time, I don't want to talk to anyone, even Ash, who I love. I know she'd only spoon-feed me sugarcoated bullshit in an attempt to make me feel better.

No. There's only one person I feel like spending time with. First name Jim, last name Beam. I can practically hear him calling my name from the liquor store up the street.

I turn my car in that direction.

If I were a smart person, I'd turn around and head back to my apartment. If I had any sense, I'd call Ash or my sponsor, and tell them what I'm about to do so they can talk me out of it.

But I've already established I'm not a smart person, and the last thing I want is to be talked out of taking a drink.

Because I need the escape from the suckpit that is reality. Just for an hour. That's all. Afterwards, maybe I can sort this mess out, come up with a new plan, or I can just keep drinking until I forget the old one.

Yep, I think, smiling to myself. Things are starting to look up already.

Chapter Twenty-Three

This was a mistake. Call it soldier's intuition. I can sense a darkness creeping over the horizon, like the first gust of wind before a hurricane.

The building pressure puts me on edge, more so than usual. My lungs swell with it, expanding my ribs to the point of breaking. I can't draw in enough air, not without exploding. I'm dizzy. My knee aches, forcing me to rely heavily on my cane. And that extra feeling of vulnerability doesn't help any.

I hate pills. But maybe, just this once, I should have taken a Xanax for this meeting—or ten.

The restaurant lobby is dark, and I keep darting my eyes to see who is hiding in the shadows. I swear something moves off to my left, and I look over my shoulder for the hundredth time. Damn it, I wish Em were here.

I don't know why she insisted on meeting me at the restaurant. Something about not wanting the motorcycle to mess up her hair, though that's never bothered her before.

Maybe she's just as nervous about meeting my parents as I am.

The restaurant, a five star Italian place—one of my parents' favorites—might have been another bad idea. While quieter than my usual pizza place, the dancing shadows cast by the candlelight play tricks with my head. I can't shake the feeling I'm being stalked.

I swallow hard, trying to ignore the relentless pounding of my pulse inside my head. I run my fingers through my hair. *Get your shit together, Reece. We're not going to do this today.*

Outside the glass doors, a white car pulls to the curb. A second later, a blonde in a tight red dress—the same color as her signature lips—steps out. *Emily. Thank God.*

She hands her keys to the valet before walking into the lobby. I start toward her, only to stop. I can't put my finger on it, but something's off. I can practically taste the wrongness of it, something sour on the back of my tongue.

"Hey." She smiles weakly and averts her eyes.

Definitely off. "Hey. Everything okay?"

Still not looking at me, she combs her fingers through her curls. "Why?"

"You didn't answer your phone when I called earlier."

"Shower," she answers shortly. The smell of mouthwash on her breath is strong. I notice the dark circles beneath her eyes she's attempted to cover with makeup.

"Did things not go well today at the coffee shop?"

"They went fine." Her smile is tight. "When are your parents supposed to get here?"

I glance at my watch. "Any minute."

"Do you think we have time for a drink?"

Now I *know* something's up. "If you're not feeling up to this, that's fine."

"Don't be ridiculous." She cranes her head toward the bar. "I wouldn't leave you—not now."

I gently grab her arm and draw her to me. "I thought you gave up drinking," I say in a hushed voice. Having her this close, I can smell a faint trace of alcohol beneath her perfume.

She squirms out of my grip. "One drink never hurt anyone."

"Em, what the hell is going on with you?"

"I'm fine," she hisses.

A man clears his throat, stopping me before I can say more. "Forgive me for interrupting," the maître d' says, looking anything but apologetic. "Your table is ready."

"Wonderful," Emily says, marching ahead of me.

The douchebag in the tuxedo appraises her as she walks by, his gaze traveling from the stud above her mouth to the tattoos decorating her arms and chest, before landing squarely on her ass. He frowns in disapproval.

My hands ball into fists before I can stop myself. *Let him say something,* I think. *Just one word.*

Lucky for his sake, he says nothing as he leads us to a table in the corner—my request—so I can keep my back to the wall. He does, however, give a slight sniff in Em's direction before walking off. Either Emily doesn't care or she doesn't notice.

I make a mental note to have a few words with Monsieur Doucheface before we leave.

Emily reaches for the wine list. Her hands tremble as she opens it.

I gently remove it from her hands. "Please talk to me."

She presses her lips together. "Not now. Later."

"Later," I echo, sliding the wine list to the far side of the table.

She nods. Her eyes lose focus as she traces circles on the tablecloth with her index finger. She's closed herself off to me. With a sinking in my gut I realize there's not a damn thing I can do to draw her out. At least not here. "We should go." I reach for my cane.

"What?" She makes a face. "We just got here, and we haven't even met your parents yet."

"Yeah, they can wait." I stand. "There's something you're not telling me. We can grab a pizza, go back to my place, and talk about it."

Her lips twitch into an almost-smile. "Actually, that sounds…" Her mouth snaps shut as her gaze narrows on something past my shoulder.

"Hello, Reece."

I haven't heard her voice in almost three years. Still, I grip the edge of the table to keep from recoiling. "Mother." I turn to face her.

She's thinner than I remember, or maybe it's just the slimming effect of her black dress. Though she still sports the same angled bob, her formerly blond hair is now almost completely white. Two large diamonds dangle from her earlobes, and her favorite pearls—a Mother's Day present from long ago—are clasped at her throat.

Dad stands beside her. Neither will look at me. Instead, they stare at my cane with matching expressions of morbid fascination.

Mother touches her throat. "It's true."

"What's true, Mom?" I ask, pulling a chair out for her. "That I'm a disabled vet? Or that I've managed to survive this long without your money?"

With wide eyes, Emily grabs onto the sleeve of a passing waiter. I can't hear what she murmurs into his ear, but I have a bad feeling it's a drink order.

Mom hesitates, turning to face Dad.

His once-dark hair is completely salt and pepper. There are more creases lining his eyes than the last time I saw him. His shoulders slump. "Son, we didn't come here to argue."

"I'm relieved to hear that," I say. "Because there's nothing to argue about."

Mom and Dad exchange a glance. Dad nods and they both sit.

After a moment, I do, too.

Mom carefully unfolds her napkin and spreads it neatly on her lap, while Dad stares at the ceiling, drumming his fingers on the table. Only when the maître d' scuttles over is the silence broken.

"Mr. and Mrs. Montgomery, I had no idea you were joining us tonight."

"Yes." Dad clears his throat. "We're here with our son."

He says nothing about Emily, or even acknowledges her existence for that matter. My blood begins to heat to lava-like temperatures.

"And Ms. Garrett," I add. "My girlfriend."

Em slumps in her chair.

Mom's head tilts sharply, like a hawk suddenly realizing the presence of a mouse. Her eyes narrow. "Your girlfriend?"

Dad's eyes narrow. "You look familiar." His eyes widen. "You're the girl from the hardware store."

The maître d' shifts uncomfortably. "I'll see to your drinks. The usual martini and scotch?"

Still staring at Emily, Mom and Dad nod.

He turns to me. "Sir?"

"Water."

He arches an eyebrow inquisitively at Emily.

She waves a hand. "I've got one on the way."

"Very good." He hurries away.

Mom's attention remains locked on Emily. "So, you're Reece's girlfriend." Her smile is stretched tight. "My, aren't you…colorful."

Before either of us can respond, the previous waiter appears and deposits an amber-colored drink in front of Emily. She hurriedly takes a sip.

"Mom." I lower my voice to a growl. "I won't let you be

rude to Emily."

"Emily," Mom repeats. Her nose scrunches, as if the name leaves a bad taste on her tongue. "How on earth was I being rude? You *are* colorful, aren't you? Isn't that the desired effect you were going for with all that…?" She gestures to Emily's tattoos.

"Ink?" Emily supplies before taking another sip. She pushes her shoulders back in that defiant way of hers I've come to love and admire. "Yes, I do love color. But tattoos are wonderful for another reason."

Mom's eyebrows raise.

"They're remarkable asshole detectors. It's amazing how clearly they allow me to spot people who are superficial, pompous asses."

This time, Mom's smile is smooth as silk. "That's nice."

Dad clears his throat. "So, Reece, tell us how you've been."

"You mean after you left me stranded, injured, and alone at the St. Louis airport? Or currently? Because the answer to both is fine."

"Reece, we were wrong," Dad admits.

His admission, so unlike him, catches me completely off guard. "What?"

"We were wrong," Mom echoes. "We were acting childish. We were punishing you for defying our wishes. Still, you're an adult and entitled to make your own decisions. We realize that, now. That's why we're here. To ask for your forgiveness."

I look at Emily to see if she's hearing the same words I am. As long as I've known my parents, they've never apologized to anyone about anything.

Em gives me a small smile accompanied by a shrug before taking another sip of her drink.

"We're so very sorry," Mom continues. "We don't blame you if you no longer want anything to do with us. But, if you're willing, we'd like to be a part of your life again."

Something inside my chest feels like it's being pulled to the point of breaking. I never realized I'd wanted their apology until now.

The waiter returns with our drink orders and offers us more time to look at the menus before scuttling away again. My head, however, is whirling so fast I'm no longer hungry.

"You don't have to say anything now," Dad says. "We're glad just for this opportunity to have dinner with you. Our treat, of course."

And there it is. I did something they liked; now they're going to reward me with money. "Don't worry about it. This one's on me."

Mom waves a hand. "Don't be ridiculous, Reece. You can't afford that on a teacher's salary. Your sister told us what you're doing now."

"You let me worry about what I can and cannot afford."

Mom opens her mouth, but Dad silences her with a look. "You're absolutely right, Son."

"While I appreciate your approval," I tell him while reaching for my water, "I'm certainly not asking for it."

Emily winks at me, a gesture that does not go unnoticed by my mother.

"We're certainly not trying to imply you need our approval," Dad says. "It appears you're doing well enough."

It's the *enough* that scratches down my skin like a fork. "What is that supposed to mean?"

"It *means*," Mom cuts in, "that we're your parents. Whether or not we're in your life, we still worry about you and want what's best for you."

"You have nothing to worry about." Emily's comment draws a frown from Mom. "Reece is fantastic."

"Are you?" Mom turns her gaze back on me. "Jessica implied you were having some difficulties—from your time in the service."

Jessica. I clench my jaw until it aches. Of course my sister, with her big mouth and need of approval, would blab everything to my parents. "I'm *fine.*"

"Darling, you have a cane. That's not the definition of fine."

"It's true. I was injured." I grip the edge of the table. "And you'd know that if you had been there to pick me up from the airport."

"It's also true," Mom counters, "you never would have been injured if you hadn't gone against our wishes and enlisted in the first place." Her lip quivers.

"Mom, I'm not Jessica. I can't just sit back and let you dictate my life for me."

"How can you say that?" She leans forward in her chair. "Though, I can't say I'm surprised. You were always accusing your father and me of controlling you. But what were we supposed to do, Reece? We're your parents. Our job is to keep you safe." Her voice trembles and her eyes swell with tears. Dad places his hand over hers. Several people from nearby tables glance in our direction.

"You call taking my trust fund away from me and cutting me out of your lives *keeping me safe?*"

Sighing, she dabs her tears away with a napkin. "So, we made a mistake. I was desperate. You were always a defiant child, and when you told me you were enlisting, I was terrified." She points to my cane. "Rightfully so."

I remain silent. There's nothing I can say to argue.

"I am your mother," she continues. "It is my job to love and protect you. I'll admit, I'm not perfect and I make mistakes." She reaches across the table and takes my hand in hers. "But as long as you are alive, I will continue to love and protect you."

Her hand is so much smaller than I remember, frail even. I want so badly to believe her. Dad gives me a hopeful smile.

Emily averts her eyes while finishing her drink. "I don't see how taking his trust fund away is protecting him," she mutters.

"How nice." Mom lets go of my hand. "She's concerned about your finances."

Emily narrows her eyes. I can practically feel the heat crackling between the two of them. "I'm *concerned* about *Reece*. He had dreamed of buying an RV and traveling the country."

"An RV?" Mom makes a face before shaking her head. "Doesn't matter. I'm glad you brought it up. As I said, that was a mistake on our part." She refocuses her attention on me. "We'd like to give it back to you."

"I told you, I don't need your money."

"It's *your* money, Son," Dad says. "It doesn't matter if you need it."

"I don't *want* it."

"Then donate it to charity." Dad waves a hand in the air. "Cash it out and set it on fire for all we care. It's yours to do whatever you like with."

For a split second, the image of my RV flashes through my head, with Emily sitting inside. I can see us driving across the country, stopping at every greasy diner and gimmicky tourist trap along the way. She'd buy a sombrero in New Mexico and I'd pick up a lobster coffee mug in New England. The dream is more than a little tempting.

Then I see Chad, his blood—along with his dream—bleeding onto the sand. I inhale sharply. RV, sombrero, and lobster coffee mug be damned. If there's a way I can use the money to rid myself of Chad's ghost, I'm going to do it. Still, I know better than to think anything from my parents would come without strings.

"What's the catch?"

Dad frowns and Mom looks taken aback.

"We told you," Mom says. "We only want you to be happy." She pauses. "*Are* you happy?"

"Sure." Even though her question catches me off guard, my answer is programmed. Automatic, even. For so long, every day was just a struggle to stay alive and happiness was a long lost dream. But that was before Emily walked into my life, bringing…color? Vibrancy? Light? Life?

Actually, she's brought all of those things.

Is that what happiness is?

A surge of panic jolts up my spine like electricity. I can't be happy. I don't deserve to be. Not when a man, barely older than a boy, gave up his life for me. *He* should be here. Chad should be happy.

"He loved motorcycles. He was going to be a veterinarian." I don't realize I've said the words out loud until I look up to find my parents staring at me with matching looks of concern.

A breeze tickles my neck, blowing sand onto my napkin. I turn to find the rest of the tables have fallen away, leaving us stranded back in the desert.

"Reece?" Emily leans forward. "Are you okay?"

In the distance, I can hear the rattle of gunfire. I reach for my gun, but it's been replaced with a useless glass of water.

A lump wedges inside my throat.

"Son? What is it?" Dad's brow furrows in concern.

I sweep my hand through my hair, already gritty with sweat and sand.

"Reece?" This voice, quieter, sounds from behind me, making me jerk back.

Turning, I find Chad stumbling toward me. Blood spurts from the slash across his neck. A chunk of his skull hangs from his head, revealing the soft pink brain inside. He stumbles to his knees beside me. "Reece?" Her voice is thick and garbled. His eyes meet mine, they're wide with fear. Already the light of life is draining from them. He teeters forward. Just before he falls I hear him ask,

"Are you happy now?"

Chapter Twenty-Four

EMILY

After his episode, Reece says very little and eats even less. When dinner's finished, I won't let him ride his motorcycle, given his state, so I drag him to my car, shove him inside, and drive his ass home.

When we arrive, I guide him into his house and steer him straight to his bedroom. "I'll take you to your bike first thing in the morning," I tell him, helping him into bed and slipping off his shoes.

He nods.

My head is beginning to throb, probably from my earlier pity party. I press my palms against my pulsing temples. "I think I might go back to my place. I'm getting a migraine, so I'm not going to be much fun."

He says nothing, only stares blankly at the wall in that way of his that lets me know he's not really with me.

"Unless…you want me to stay?" I add.

He blinks then, his eyes focusing before finding mine.

"Maybe you should stay. Maybe you should stay forever."

I snort, sure I've heard him wrong. "Go to sleep. You're delusional."

"I'm serious." He sits up. "I've been carrying all this guilt around for so long, guilt that my life will never amount to the life Chad should have had. But maybe I can do better."

I never know what Reece I'm going to get after he has a panic attack. Usually, it's sleepy Reece. Sometimes, it's paranoid Reece. Tonight, I got super-ambitious-I-need-to-make-changes Reece. I cross my arms. It's my least favorite Reece. "What are you talking about?"

He peels the covers back and swings his legs out of bed. "Maybe if I make my life mean something, Chad wouldn't have died for nothing."

"Sweetie, Chad *didn't* die for nothing. You aren't nothing. I hate it when you say that."

He waves a hand in the air. "Listen, I can go back to law school and become a lawyer. I might not be able to fight physically, but I can do it in the courtroom. I can make a difference."

I knew something happened to him at the restaurant, but this episode is unlike any I've dealt with before. "Reece, you *do* make a difference. Every day at school. Besides, you're done fighting, remember?"

"That's what a coward would say."

"You told me yourself you would hate being a lawyer."

"Yes." He nods. "But at least I'd be doing something worthwhile."

"This is insane." I throw my arms in the air. "You need sleep. In the morning you're going to realize how insane this all is."

"It's not." He limps toward me and takes my hands in his. "I've spent all these years wasting my life. I have to make it count for something. For Chad." He pauses. "I think we should get married."

I yank my hands out of his. "As romantic as that proposal was, I think you've lost your mind."

"No." He shakes his head. "I think I'm actually seeing things clearly."

"How so?"

"I've been carrying this terrible guilt for so long. But what if I didn't have to? What if I changed, made my life more meaningful?"

"And you think getting married is the answer?"

"Why waste time? I think if we're not moving forward, we're not moving at all. Don't I make you happy?"

"Of course, but—"

"Then what are we waiting for?"

"Reece, you had a bad attack in the restaurant, and you're still not thinking clearly. I'm sure you'll agree in the morning, after a good night's sleep."

"Emily." He grabs my hand. "I need my life to count."

"Your life already counts. Why can't you see that?"

"What's the big deal?" he asks. "Marriage is the natural progression of relationships."

"Says who?" I counter. "Where the hell is all this coming from?"

He drops my hand. "You don't want to get married."

"Of course I don't want to get married. I'm not the one having a mental breakdown, Reece."

He takes a step backward. It's such a small step, but the distance between us feels like it's expanding by the second. "Do you *ever* want to get married?"

"I don't know." Hugging my arms to my body, I turn away. "It feels like such an outdated institution, you know? We have something good going right now, why mess it up?"

"So, you're saying commitment messes relationships up?"

"I don't know. I'm just saying maybe marriage isn't for

me." I run my fingers through my hair. God, why are we even having this conversation?

"You don't want to get married? Ever?"

"I don't know."

"Emily, you have to know. This is important."

"Why? Does it make a difference?"

He's silent a moment. "I think so, yes. I need to know we're not screwing around. That this is going somewhere."

"Why does it have to go somewhere to mean something? Things are great the way they are."

"Except they're not."

I stare at him.

"I want more," he says.

"I don't. At least…at least, not right now."

His eyes flood with hurt. "I'm not enough?"

"Damn it, Reece. *I'm* not enough. My boss wouldn't give me a chance because she doesn't believe I can handle responsibility. Hell, maybe she's right. Maybe I'm just a fuckup who's destined to *remain* a fuckup for the rest of her life. But I refuse to get married because I have nothing else going for me."

Surprise flashes across his face. "I'm sorry you had a setback, Em. I really am. But how can you call what we have nothing?"

I rake my fingers through my hair. "We're not nothing, Reece, but we're also not…enough. Why can't you understand that?"

"The way I see it, there's nothing to understand." His jaw flexes. "You've just been screwing with me this whole time, haven't you? Literally, huh?"

Hurt wrenches my heart. "How can you say that?"

"I should have known." He inhales sharply. "You said no strings attached. I was too stupid to listen."

"Reece, you're not even giving me a chance."

"No." His head snaps up. "*You're* not giving *us* a chance, Emily. And I've wasted enough time. I can't waste any more."

I hear every word out of his mouth, but it's like my brain can't make sense of it. "You're saying if I don't agree to marry you, we're done."

"I don't need you to agree to marry me now, but I need to know it's in the future. Is it?"

I'm losing him. I can feel him slipping away like water through my fingers. It would be so easy to lie. So easy to tell him, of course I can picture us getting married someday. But the truth is I don't even know what tomorrow will bring, let alone months down the road.

His shoulders hunch. "I guess I have my answer."

Tears well in my eyes, blurring my vision. As much as they burn, I refuse to blink. I won't let them fall. "You're not being fair."

"Grow up, Emily." His words hit me like a slap in the face. They're the words I've heard nonstop from my brother and mother the last couple of years. "You're not a child anymore. It's time to figure out what you want."

"You're right." I snatch my clutch off his dresser. "At least I've figured out one thing—I know I don't want a man who gives me ultimatums." I shuffle inside my purse for my keys. "And I don't want to be here a second longer."

I leave his bedroom and head for the door. Without turning, I feel him following me. Every cell in my body pulls toward him, aching to hear him call out my name and admit he's made a big mistake.

But that moment never comes.

Chapter Twenty-Five

REECE

I stare at the door for ten minutes after she leaves, sure she's going to come back. She doesn't.

While part of me feels like my heart has been ripped in two, another part is relieved. I can't figure out why. The first—and only—woman I could picture spending my life with just walked out the door. How sick in the head am I to actually be even a little okay with that?

I tell myself it's a good thing I cut Emily loose sooner than later—especially if she's just screwing around with me. But another voice, a much smaller one, says maybe I feel better because the one person who makes me happy is gone.

Because I don't deserve to be happy.

Not yet, anyway. Not until I set my life right. Chad had a goal. His life would have had meaning. I might actually be able to rid myself of the guilt if I can do the same.

Every footstep is a struggle. I'm tired. More tired than I can ever remember being in my entire life. I sit on the edge of my bed and let my head fall into my hands. Thoroughly exhausted, I feel empty, hollowed out.

Em must have taken part of me with her when she walked out the door. I was already broken, but now I'm less—less a person, less a man—than I was five minutes ago.

How does a person recover after that? How do they continue on?

What the hell have I done?

Chapter Twenty-Six

EMILY

The first thing I do when I get home is pour a drink. Earlier, after my boss rejected my business plan, I actually felt guilty purchasing the big bottles of Jim Beam and Belvedere now sitting on my coffee table.

My first sip came with the tiniest twinge of remorse. And maybe that was shame burning through my veins after I finished the first glass.

But now, tipping back another glass and swallowing the contents in one long gulp, I feel absolutely nothing.

Well, maybe not nothing.

I pour a second glass and a flicker of anger ignites within my chest. By the fourth glass, it's an all-out raging inferno.

It's not Reece I'm pissed at but myself. Because I knew better.

I knew the risks of getting involved with someone. I knew the trap, and still, I walked right in.

Even more than that, I'm pissed at how much pain I feel.

Because it only proves how much I let my guard down.

I tip another drink back. My fifth? Sixth? Who knows? The room is beginning to wobble, and I'm finally, *finally,* going numb. Thank God, too. Because no matter how big the hangover will be in the morning, it won't compare to the pain I felt when I walked out the door.

While he just silently stood by and let me.

Chapter Twenty-Seven

REECE

I fucked up. I realize it the second my alarm goes off, reach over, and find the spot beside me cold and empty. Last night was not another horrible nightmare. Last night, my girl—the best thing that ever happened to me—walked out my front door.

Slowly, I pull myself out of bed as the events replay in my mind.

I was sure Em and I were headed somewhere.

She wasn't.

If two people have any chance of ending up at the same destination, they at least need to be walking the same path. And we're not. Pure and simple.

But if this is the right thing, the best thing, why does it feel so wrong?

Before I can stop myself, I grab my phone and dial Em's number. Her voicemail picks up after the first ring. She's probably already at work. Muttering a curse, I take a quick shower, shave, and dress. Minutes later I'm at the coffee shop.

But for the first time since we've been together, Em isn't.

Alice, Em's boss, smiles at me from behind the counter when I walk in. "The usual Americano?" Some young guy hands a steaming cup to a waiting customer. It slips from his fingers, splattering coffee and foam across the floor.

"Not today. I was looking for Em."

Alice frowns. "She called in sick. I thought you knew."

"No. But thanks." I don't offer any more explanation before heading for the door. Honestly, I'm not sure what I know anymore.

I don't have enough time to stop at Em's apartment before school. But when the last bell rings, I'm out the door before the kids and on my bike before the first bus pulls out. I still don't know what I'm going to say to Em when I see her. Knowing that we're not wasting each other's time is important to me, but at the same time, I did go about it the wrong way.

I'm man enough to admit I lost my fucking mind last night.

I just hope I haven't fucked things up for good.

I'm at her apartment in record time. Her car's not parked in its usual spot outside the building, but I knock on her door anyway.

She doesn't answer.

Since I left my cane at home, I'm forced to hobble back to my bike like the defeated asshole I am.

I keep my phone close by in case Em decides to call.

She doesn't.

And she doesn't the next day, either. Or the day after.

With each passing day that I don't see Emily, panic swells inside my chest like an overinflated balloon on the verge of bursting. It's always the same. She doesn't answer my calls, she's absent from work, and she's never at her apartment.

After a week, I'm desperate. I dig out the card Lane gave

me in the hospital and dial the number.

"Hello?" The voice is familiar, and distinctively not male.

"Ashlyn?"

There's a pause, followed by, "Who is this?"

"It's Reece."

She inhales sharply.

"I take it Emily told you what happened."

"Did you really ask her to marry you?" Ashlyn asks.

"I had a freak out. Listen, I need to talk to her. She hasn't been at work. She won't answer my calls. And she's never at her apartment. Do you have any idea where I can find her?"

Ashlyn doesn't answer.

"Please?" I ask. "I know I fucked up."

"You really did," she says. "Em's only twenty-one. For you to put that kind of pressure on her was a real asshole move."

"I know. That's why I need to talk to her—to fix my fuckup."

Ashlyn is quiet for several heartbeats before finally sighing. "Fine. There's a bar she used to hang out at—the Wishing Well. She's really good friends with the bartender. I bet you'll find her there."

"Thanks, Ashlyn. I'm going to make this right." After saying good-bye, I hang up, grab my keys, and hop onto my bike.

I pull my bike next to several others already parked outside the Wishing Well. The bass thumps so loudly I can feel it in the soles of my boots as I walk toward the bar. When I reach the filthy glass door, I hesitate. Through smeared nicotine, I can see a crowd of thrashing dancers writhing to God-awful music inside.

At the very idea of pushing through a crowd that thick,

my throat tightens. There's no telling where an enemy might be hiding. Any one of the people grinding against each other could have a gun, or worse, and explosives strapped to their chest.

Fuck. Maybe I should just go home.

But then I see a flash of platinum hair tied with a red bandana, bobbing through the heads at the front of the stage, and I know there's no going back.

Swallowing the jagged lump that's pushed up my throat, I open the door and step inside.

I wince from the audible assault that's supposed to be music. I make it two steps into the bar when the first asshole bumps into me. Reflexively, every muscle in my body tightens, and it takes all of my strength to unclench my fists. I can do this. I *will* do this. For Em.

"Reece!"

I turn in the direction of the voice. Tonya waves me over from a table beside the wall.

Before I head over, I survey the crowd for Em's red bandana. But I lost it in the sea of bodies. Tonya's table is close to the door. At least there, Em won't be able to leave without me seeing her.

Sitting on a barstool, dressed in jeans and a tank top, Tonya smiles when I approach. "What the hell is Reece Montgomery doing in a place like this?"

"I could ask you the same thing," I answer, still searching the crowd.

Tonya makes a face. "You know Lexi, my student teacher? This was all her idea. She begged me to come out because this band was *so amazing*." She makes quotes with her fingers. "I guess I really am getting old, because these guys sound like somebody stuffed a bag full of cats and ran over them...with a Zamboni."

I can't help but crack a smile. "Nice visual."

She shrugs. "I'd rather be at Mac's watching the game. Instead, I'm stuck here babysitting." She gestures to the crowd, and I spot Lexi grinding against some baby-faced guy with his pants hanging halfway down his ass.

"Is he even old enough to be in a bar?" I ask.

Tonya drums her nails on the table. "Don't know. Don't care. What I do find interesting, however, is solving the mystery of what the hell you're doing here."

"No mystery. Emily's here." I nod to the dancing mob. "Somewhere in there."

Tonya arches an eyebrow. "The mysterious Emily is *here*?" She hops off her barstool. "Where? I've been dying to meet the girl who put a smile on Sergeant Scowl's face."

"What the hell did you just call me?"

She tilts her head. "You didn't know that's what the kids call you?"

"You're making that up."

She pats my arm. "Whatever helps you sleep at night, Sarge."

I grunt. "Doesn't matter. What does is getting the hell out of here. I need to find Em."

"I'll help," Tonya offers. "What does she look like?"

"Short, platinum blond hair, red bandana, tattoos."

"Really?" Tonya's eyes widen. "*That's* your type? No wonder I didn't stand a chance."

I wave her words away. "Are you going to help me or not?"

"Chill. I'll help." She returns to her barstool and holds out a hand. "Help me up."

Taking her hand, I help her climb on top of the table. Squinting her eyes, she surveys the crowd. Her lips move, but I can't hear what she's mumbling over the noise coming off the stage. Her head moves back and forth until finally, her eyes widen. Even though I can't hear her, the word "fuck" is unmistakable on her lips.

Tonya quickly climbs off the table. "This was probably a bad idea."

Ice fills my chest. "What is it?"

She waves a hand in the air. "Couldn't find her. And you know what? I'm tired of babysitting. I bet we can still catch the last inning of the game if we head over to Mac's. Wanna go?"

She's lying. I can see it with each dart of her eyes and nervous wringing of her hands. "What aren't you telling me?"

Tonya bites her lip.

"Fine. I'll find her myself." Hobbling to the edge of the crowd, I'm not gentle when I shove people out of the way. With every nerve in my body on high alert, I'm past the point of caring.

Following the flashes of red, it doesn't take me long to find her.

Even shorter is the realization I wish I hadn't.

Some skinny dirtbag wearing a mesh trucker hat stands behind her, with his hands on her hips. She leans her back against his chest, one arm around his neck, as he grinds against her so hard, they'd be fucking if it wasn't for the fabric separating them.

The floor slips out from under my feet, and I'm falling. At least it feels that way. I move forward, hands clenched into fists. I don't know what I'm going to do when I get my hands on that greasy little fucker, and I don't care. My body's switched to military mode, which means react first, think later.

Before I can reach them, a hand wraps around my arm and yanks me back. I whirl around, prepared to fight an enemy. Instead, I find Tonya.

Whatever look is on my face, it makes fear flash through Tonya's eyes. To her credit, she doesn't let go. "Reece, don't do anything stupid. Let's just get out of here, okay?"

I turn back to Emily. She's still dancing. Eyes closed and smiling. She spins around, facing the prick, straddling his leg as she runs her hands through her hair.

I taste bile on my tongue. Or maybe that's just the flavor of rage. I try and move toward her, but Tonya tightens her hold.

"Reece." Her tone has changed. She's no longer asking. "We're leaving. Now." When I make no move to budge, she repeats, "*Now*."

The fierceness in her voice sounds too much like an order for me to disobey. Tonya puts her arm around my waist. With my muscles still coiled and shoulders tight, I allow her to steer me toward the exit.

I pause only when we reach the door. I look back toward the crowd, and it could be my imagination, but I swear I see her face through the moving bodies, watching me. Even if she was, what would it matter? I came here to win her back. But it's apparent I'm too late.

She's already moved on.

Chapter Twenty-Eight

I'm drunk. But since I'm only on my second drink, there's no way that's possible. Unless someone slipped me something. If that were the case, wouldn't I feel all dizzy and sleepy and shit? I'm hot, very sweaty, a little tired, but overall, fine.

So why am I seeing visions of Reece? Wishful thinking? I mean, there's no way he would venture into a crowded noisy place like this. He'd have an attack before he set foot through the door. Still, every so often, I glimpse a tall, blond-haired guy through gaps in the crowd.

I stop dancing.

Eddie, a friend of mine from high school, releases my hips. "What's wrong?"

I shake my head. "This sounds crazy, but I swear I saw my ex-boyfriend."

"Is that okay?" He puts an arm protectively around my shoulder. "Do you need me to walk you out?"

I pat his hand. "That's sweet. But it's not like that. I'll be fine."

He frowns in disbelief. "You sure?"

"Yeah."

"Okay." He takes his arm off my shoulder. "I'm going to ask that cute guy over there to dance." He points to a bearded redhead standing alone by the stage. "If you're not back by the end of the next song, I'm going to come find you."

"Deal. Good luck."

Eddie winks before ducking around a dancing couple on his way to the stage.

I head toward the door, only to stop after a couple of feet.

His usual sport coat has been replaced with a leather jacket, but there's no mistaking that body, or the slight limp when he moves, despite not using his cane today. He's talking to someone I can't see through the crowd of dancers. What the hell is he doing here?

"Reece!" I call out. He doesn't look up. Must not be able to hear me over the music. I walk toward him just in time to see a pretty brunette slide her arm around his waist and guide him to the door.

I gasp, feeling like I've just been punched in the gut. My heart falls from my chest, sliding all the way to my ankles.

The brunette looks every bit like the type of girl he should be with. Long, straight hair, boring makeup, and not a tattoo in sight. I bet she was in a sorority. She probably owns several strands of pearls.

She grabs the door handle, but Reece hesitates. Turning, our eyes meet. He holds my gaze for several seconds, then turns and walks out the door.

My stomach clenches so tight I'm sure my whiskey is going to make reappearance. I stumble to the bar. My hands are shaking as I flag Ren over. "I need a drink," I gasp.

Ren frowns. "Honey, I know breakups are hard, but you've been drowning your sorrows in booze for a week straight. Maybe it's time to ease up."

I grab the edge of the bar so tightly my knuckles turn white. My throat is so tight I can barely breathe. "Tonight is not the night to take it easy. Drink. Please."

Ren's face softens. "Did something happen?"

"He was here." I lick my suddenly dry lips. "With another girl. The asshole looked right at me and pretended I didn't exist."

Ren says nothing, only grabs a glass and fills it with two finger-widths of Crown. Before handing it to me, she mutters, "What the hell," and makes it a double.

"Thank you so much." My entire body is trembling when I take the drink. I tip it back in one long swallow. Immediately, comforting warmth blankets my insides. The trembling lessens. "You better keep these coming."

Ren frowns. "Okay. But just for tonight."

"Just for tonight," I echo.

Ren starts to leave and I snag her wrist. "If it's all right with you, can I stay at your place again? I'm not ready to be alone—not yet."

Ren nods. "Sure, honey."

I let go of her hand. She glides down the opposite end of the bar, snagging two beers along the way.

I know Eddie will be wondering what happened to me, but I can't go back on the dance floor. I feel as if my heart's been pummeled with a jackhammer. Every intake of breath hurts. Blinking hurts. Existing hurts.

I reach for my glass and lick the few remaining drops of whiskey.

At least I know exactly how to chase away the pain.

Chapter Twenty-Nine

REECE

The bar patrons cheer in unison at some play I missed because I'm too busy watching the condensation trickle down my beer bottle. I glance at the television to see the replay. With a bases-loaded homerun, the Cardinals have taken the lead.

I can't bring myself to care even a little bit.

Tonya frowns at me from the barstool to my right. "Why are you even here, Reece?"

I shake my head and pick at the corner of the beer label. It's been two months since I spotted Emily with another guy at the bar. While Tonya's taken me out nearly every weekend since, she's been unable to break through the numb haze surrounding me. "I have no idea."

She snorts before taking a long swig of her beer. When she's finished, she sets her beer down and mumbles, "God, men are idiots."

I glare at her. "What?"

"Men are idiots," she repeats, loud enough that several

nearby men turn to scowl at her. The bartender, on the other hand, nods. "You've been nothing but miserable for the last two months. *Call her.*"

"I'm not going to call her. She moved on. You saw it yourself, remember?"

Tonya rolls her eyes. "You don't know that. That guy could have been just a friend."

"Friends don't dance like that."

She makes a disgusted sound. "You're a moron."

I take a sip of my beer. It's warm. "Why the hell am I friends with you?"

"Because nobody else would put up with you."

I shrug, because I know it's true. My mood swings and anxiety have only increased since Emily left. Even now, I'm afraid to look anywhere but at my lukewarm beer, out of fear I'll see Chad in the shadows, scowling at me, eyes narrowed with accusation.

A manifestation of my guilt, my therapist says. *Not real,* he reminds me during our visits. I had to increase them thanks to my insomnia and increasing panic attacks. Ghost or guilt, it doesn't really matter, because he feels real. That's what keeps me up at night.

"Call her," Tonya repeats.

I grunt. "I'm not going to harass her. She doesn't want me."

"She doesn't want to get married." Tonya pokes my chest with her finger. "That's different from not wanting you."

"Maybe." With one swipe, I rip the label off my beer and crumple it in my hand. "If she loved me, *really loved me,* why would she have moved on so fast?"

"How do you know she moved on?"

I make a face and take another sip of my beer.

"You're being unreasonable," Tonya says.

"I know what I want. I don't have time to waste for

someone to get their shit together."

She tips the neck of her beer at me. "Dude, you're only twenty-eight."

"Exactly. And I haven't done shit to show for it."

"Reece, you fought for our country and lived to tell the tale. Now you're a teacher, molding the minds of future generations. You've done more than most people do in a lifetime."

I turn away and focus on my beer. "It's not enough."

The bar erupts into another round of cheering. I flinch.

"Okay, then." Tonya's voice is softer, soothing even. "What *will* make it enough?"

"I don't know," I mutter then take another swig. A shadow shifts behind me. I won't—*can't*—look. I'm too afraid it'll be Chad staring at me as his life bleeds out of his neck. "Sometimes I think nothing will."

"I don't believe that." She shakes her head.

I make a face. It doesn't matter what she believes, it's not her truth to face. "You don't know what happened."

"I don't have to," she counters. "Whatever it was, you don't deserve a life of misery."

I slam my bottle down so hard beer sloshes over the lip and runs down my fingers. "I don't deserve a life at all. It should be him here. Not me."

She touches me, her fingers sliding over mine. Her hands are larger than Emily's, her fingers more delicate. Noticing the differences, I realize how badly I miss Emily's touch. "You are exactly where you're supposed to be."

"Why?" My voice cracks.

"I'll help you figure that out." She hesitates. "I bet if Emily were here, she'd help, too."

"No. I'm too damaged, too fucked up, Tonya. She's better off without me."

"And there it is." She releases my hand and motions to

the bartender to bring us two more beers. "I wondered how long it would take you to finally admit it."

"What?" I ask.

"The real reason you pushed her away."

Before I can respond, the bartender sets another beer in front of me. I push the old beer aside and take a long draw on the cold one. "It's the truth," I finally mutter.

"No." She places her hand on my wrist. "She's not better off without you. She loved you, Reece. And you loved her."

Silent, I pick at the corner of the new beer's label. "Even so," I say finally, "it doesn't matter. She's gone. And I'm still fucked up."

"You are fucked up," she agrees. "But Emily doesn't have to be gone…at least, not forever."

I grunt. "What the hell does that mean?"

She swivels to face me. "Take it from someone who's dated her fair share of losers. You can't be in a relationship until you have your shit together. And you, my friend, do not have your shit together."

"Didn't I just say that?"

"But what if you did?" she asks. "I mean, there's not a person alive who has all their shit together, but what if you got like…seventy-five percent of it together?"

"What?"

"Okay, you're right. That may be too optimistic. Sixty-five?"

I snort. "And how do you propose I do that?"

"I don't know." She shrugs. "But I'm willing to help you figure it out." She pauses. "On one condition."

"And that is?"

"Afterward, you call Emily."

"I already tried that."

"So, you'll try again."

I wave a hand in the air. "Whatever. *Sure*. It doesn't

matter anyway."

"What's that supposed to mean?" she asks.

"It means your naïve confidence that I can be fixed is adorable."

She scowls. "I'm not trying to *fix* you, you idiot. And I'm not naïve enough to think that can happen overnight. But I'm willing to help you find the path that sets you in the right direction."

I roll my eyes and take another long draw from my beer bottle. "You do that."

"I will. And then you have to call Emily."

"And then I'll call Emily." I agree because I know, without a doubt, that will never happen. There's no fixing me. And there's sure as hell no path in that direction. The desert is as much a part of me now as my blood. Each beat of my heart pushes it deeper inside me.

Tonya's right about one thing, though. I am an idiot. Or at least, I was. Thinking, even for a moment, I could have a normal life with a normal relationship. Maybe asking Emily to marry me was my way of pushing her away. Still, she's better off.

Emily is vibrant, too full of life for me to let my darkness infect her. The only path I walk is one littered with death, blood, and ghosts. That's one path I'm determined to walk alone.

Chapter Thirty

Emily

"You're cut off." Ren scoops the pyramid of empty shot glasses up from in front of me and deposits them into a bin for washing.

"You can't do that." I blink at my cell phone, trying to make sense of the numbers blurred on the screen. "It's only six o'clock."

Ren folds her arms across her chest. "It's nine o'clock. Not that the time matters. You're trashed."

"You can't tell me what to do."

She laughs. "Actually, it's my bar, so I can."

"I'm an adult." The words come out whinier than I intend.

"Really?" She takes a step toward me. "You sure as hell haven't been acting like one."

I wrinkle my nose—or at least, I think I do. Honestly, I can't really feel my face. "What the hell is that supposed to mean?"

"It *means* I'm tired of you ending each day shit-faced in

my bar. That's not grownup-like behavior."

"Screw you. I thought bartenders liked it when people drank in their establishments. Whatever. I can take my money elsewhere."

I try to stand, but the ground wavers beneath my feet. I clutch the bar top to keep upright.

"You're not going anywhere." Ren grabs my keys. "I called your brother. He's on his way to pick you up."

"I don't need my keys. I can call an Uber." I reach for my phone, but Ren swipes it from under my fingers. "Bitch."

Ren's face darkens. "I'm going to ignore that, honey, because this isn't you. But I have to warn you, my patience is wearing thin."

I plop back down on the barstool. "I guess you don't really know me at all, then. Because this is exactly who I am."

Ren raises an eyebrow. "How's that?"

"Drunken, directionless, loser. That's who everybody thinks I am. I'm just living up to expectations."

Ren leans across the bar and takes my hands in hers. "That is *not* who you are."

I grunt and withdraw my hands from hers. "Shows what you know."

Ren leans back with a sigh. Her eyes drift toward the door. "We can get a second opinion if you like."

I follow her gaze to see Ashlyn walking toward me, her brow creased with lines of worry.

A tangle of guilt winds through my gut. I know I'm the one that put those lines there.

"Emily, what's going on?" Ash asks, swinging her purse onto the bar top and settling onto the stool beside me. "Ren called and…" She inhales deeply. "You're just lucky I talked your brother into staying home."

I shrug. "You should have let him come. What's the worst he can do? Yell at me? Tell me stuff I already know?"

Ash leans back. "So it's a pity party, then?"

"Yeah, so? Throwing pity parties is just another one of my endearing qualities. Like being a loser."

She makes a face. "You are *not* a loser."

"Tell that to Lane. Tell that to my boss at the coffee house. Tell that to…Reece." I nearly choke on his name, forcing me to look away. It's been almost three days since I last thought about him. Maybe weeks since I spoke his name out loud. God, saying it after all this time hurts just as bad as when I said it the night he was here in the bar…and he turned and walked away.

"Em," Ash's voice is softer. She places a hand on my shoulder. "You can't keep going on like this. I love you too much to let you self-destruct. So do your mother and Lane."

I stare at the empty pile of shot glasses in the dish tub. All of them are mine. "A person can't change," I tell her. "Why can't any of you understand that? Why does everyone want me to be something—*someone*—that I'm not?"

"This *isn't* you," Ash says.

"How do you know?"

"Because you're my best friend." She smiles. "I know exactly how smart you are. How clever and funny. You're an amazing aunt to Harper, a loving sister to Lane, and you're the sister I never had."

For reasons I don't understand, her words burn, forcing me to look away.

"Em, you're drowning in a sea of self-loathing and alcohol. You were there for me when I had nobody. Let me be here for you."

I shake my head. "You can't help me."

She's quiet for a moment before answering, "Maybe not. But I can take you to people who can."

I snap my head up. "There's no way in hell you're going to make me go to rehab."

"You're right." She nods. "I can't make you. But I can drive you there. I can hold your hand when you walk inside. And I'll be waiting to take you home when you're ready."

What feels like a thousand emotions collide inside me, creating a massive explosion. Hurt. Anger. Betrayal. Fear. "You can't make me go," I whisper.

"I've already packed you a bag. It's in the car right now. We can go tonight. All I need you to do is say yes."

A wedge of emotion lodges inside my throat. It takes me several moments before I'm able to speak. "I don't want to go."

She places a hand on my arm. This time I make no move to remove it. "Sometimes what we want and what we need are two different things."

I think about that, making a list of all the things I thought I wanted. Fun. Travel. No commitments. No strings. But have any of those given me fulfillment? Were any of those what I needed?

"Are you ready?" Ash slides off the barstool and extends a hand toward me.

I stare at it for several heartbeats. If I take her hand, things will change. Maybe for the better—maybe for the worse. If I don't take it, I get to keep my life exactly the way it is.

Which is what? Aimless? Lonely? Awful?

"What will happen to me if I go?" I ask.

Ash smiles, leaving her hand waiting in the air. "I don't know. But don't you want to find out?"

I do, I realize, as I close my hand around hers.

I really do.

Chapter Thirty-One

EMILY

I hate therapy. I hate therapy. I hate therapy.

It's all I can think as I sit down in the plush arm chair across from the therapist. Well, that and how much I'd like to kill Ash and Lane for making me come here.

The therapist is an older woman, definitely a former hippie, with her bare feet, ankle-length skirt, and earrings that touch her shoulders.

"Emily." She climbs onto a chair across from me, tucking her feet underneath her. "If it's all right, I'd like to retouch on something you brought up yesterday—your grandmother."

I grunt and let my head fall back against the chair. She doesn't screw around—just dives right into my brain and pokes around with a fork.

Mary, the therapist, only smiles at my obvious reluctance. "She was the one that got you into baking, correct?"

I roll my eyes. "You already know the answer to this. We've been talking about it all week."

Smiling, she jots down a note on her pad. I can't piss this woman off, and it drives me absolutely insane. Pissing people off is a talent of mine—practically a superpower—and this woman is immune. "Right," Mary continues, "and you mentioned your boss at the coffee shop rejected your baking proposal. That must have hurt especially bad. It must have seemed like she rejected you, and your grandmother as well."

I pause before I answer. "Maybe..."

Mary sets her notepad aside and leans forward. I fight the urge to shrink back. "What if I told you, I think you rejected your grandmother before your boss ever had the chance?"

I jerk back like I've been struck. "I'd call you a crazy bitch."

To my annoyance, Mary's grin only widens.

"I loved my grandmother more than anything," I add.

Mary laces her fingers together. "I'm not talking about love, Emily. I'm sure you loved her a great deal. I'm talking about authenticating her and, therefore, authenticating yourself."

I run my face with my hands. "Are you even trying to make sense right now? Or is driving people insane with psychobabble a fun game for you."

Mary laughs. "I can't make your self-discovery for you, Emily. You're going to have to work with me here."

Sighing, I drop my hands.

"You keep telling me in our therapy sessions together, you don't know what to do with your life. But it's obvious that's not true. The baking you did with your grandmother— that's your passion, right?"

"It was," I mutter. "But it wasn't meant to be."

"No." She shakes her head. "Maybe the cookies and cupcakes aren't meant to be. But what about the *real* baking your grandmother did. The other things you told me about?"

"Like the *baba* and honey cakes?" I snort. "Americans

wouldn't like that stuff."

"Do you?"

"I love it. But I grew up on it."

Mary retrieves her discarded notebook. Without looking at me, she adds, "So who doesn't have faith in her grandmother, now?"

I lean back, so stunned by her revelation I can't speak.

"I just want you to think about it," Mary says, her voice low and soothing. "It's not the American desserts your grandmother loved. It was the food from her homeland. That's where her spirit is. That's where her passion was. And I have a hunch, that's where you'll find yours, too." She clicks her pen closed and sets it aside.

"What if you're wrong?" I think about all the shit I've been through in the last year, from the car accident, to being rejected at work, to Reece giving me the ultimatum. "I don't think I can survive another rejection."

She laughs at this. "Of course you can. You're a hell of a strong woman, Emily. What you can't survive is going down this path of drinking and self-loathing. I'm only presenting you with one path of many that could lead to your happiness. Don't you think you owe it to yourself to explore your options?"

Again, I think about Reece, and how he walked away from me. And I did nothing except watch him go. Would things have been different if I hadn't given up so easily? If I'd fought for myself instead of running away?

"What if it's too late?"

Mary shakes her head. "The only time it's too late is when you're dead. You, Emily, are still very much alive."

Chapter Thirty-Two

REECE

The flashes of cameras flood my vision with spots. Goose, the black Labrador at my side, noses my clenched fist, alerting me to my rising anxiety. I exhale slowly, the way my therapist instructed, and scratch the back of Goose's ear.

The bands of anxiety around my chest loosen just a fraction. It's enough that I can breathe, and that's all I need to get through this moment until the next.

Goose glances up at me. I can read the worry in her eyes as plainly as if they were human. I smile back, hoping to convey I'm okay—at least for right now.

I was originally resistant to the idea of a PTSD service dog when my therapist first suggested it. But now, standing on a stage at the University of Illinois—farther from my home than I've been since the desert—I don't know how I would have traveled here without her.

Five young kids, practically babies—God, is that what I looked like when I went off to war?—line up in front of me.

Skinny and zit-faced, their hands shake as they accept the envelope I hand them with their checks inside.

"Congratulations," I mutter, shaking each sweaty hand before turning, plastering on a smile, and posing for the obligatory photo op.

"Thank you so much for this opportunity." This from the smiling redhead at the end of the line. "I wouldn't be able to attend veterinary college if not for this scholarship."

Opportunity. The word echoes inside my brain. Something Chad never had, but now, because of the foundation I set up in his name, others will.

It's not enough. It will never be enough.

But it's something.

When the awards ceremony ends, Goose and I linger at the back of the auditorium, waiting for the crowd to filter out before I make my getaway. It took all I had just to climb on that stage. I doubt I have the energy to stand for even one more photo.

"Excuse me."

So much for getting away unnoticed. I turn and find a woman roughly my mother's age. Her black hair is streaked with silver. Her floral dress hangs loosely on her shoulders. Her fingers work nervously, twisting a ring around and around on her finger. There's something familiar about her, some piece to a puzzle I didn't even know I was missing.

"I traveled from Mississippi to be here," she says. "I *had* to be here. My son—"

"Chad," I blurt. I look into her eyes and see *his* eyes stare back at me.

Goose shifts nervously beside me, her tail beating a frantic rhythm against my leg. Absently, I reach for her ear and stroke it.

"Yes," she answers and gives me a small smile. "My youngest. The only boy out of five children." She stops twisting her ring.

I want to run, but my feet are somehow glued to the spot. I brace myself for her accusations, for her hatred and rage. I failed her son. God knows I deserve whatever she gives me.

She touches my arm, and it's all I can do not to flinch. "I wanted to come here…I had to tell you in person. Thank you."

My throat is so tight it takes me several tries before I'm able to swallow. Maybe a lack of oxygen is screwing with my brain. I'm sure I heard her wrong. "Please, don't thank me."

She frowns and drops her arm. "What?"

"Please, don't thank me. Don't *ever* thank me. I failed your son."

Her face softens. "Oh, honey, no. War killed my boy. Not you."

"But if only I—"

"Listen," she cuts me off. "Chad loved you. Told me you were like the brother he never had. Talked about you all the time when we had our computer visits."

Her words do something to me. I can feel myself cracking from the inside.

She grabs my hands suddenly, squeezing them nearly to the point of pain. Goose whines and nudges my leg with her nose. It's her way of alerting me to my rising anxiety— something I realized completely on my own.

"It's true. I don't know exactly what happened or how. But I saw my baby when he returned to me. I made them open his coffin. A mother has to be sure—I *had* to be sure. It was him." Her voice catches. "My baby. You didn't do those things. You didn't kill my boy."

I open my mouth, but she cuts me off with a shake of her head. "This foundation is a wonderful thing you're doing. But you can't hold onto my boy any longer. Chad wouldn't want that. You need to let him go."

Maybe it's because the words are coming from Chad's mother, or maybe it's because they have the same eyes, but they do something to me. I can feel the crack inside me widening, accompanied by a flood of pain. My eyes well with tears that I've been holding back for five long years.

I crumple in the woman's arms. She's so much smaller than me—so much frailer—yet she has the strength to hold me up. How? How can she be so strong?

"Shhh," she whispers, her hands stroking circles on my back. "It's time to let him go. It's time to let it all go."

I want to tell her I don't know how to, or even if I can. What if she's wrong? What if Chad doesn't want to be let go? I look up, sure I'll see him standing in the shadows. Always behind me. Always near.

But this time, no matter where I look, he's nowhere to be seen.

That night, Goose watches me flip a burger on the small charcoal grill outside my new, pre-owned Winnebago Minnie Winnie. It's not the full size RV of my dreams, but it's all I could afford after donating the bulk of my trust fund to set up Chad's veterinary scholarship foundation. And honestly, it has a bed, shower, toilet, and gets me where I'm going. I don't need anything else.

But that's not exactly true.

There are times—night is the worst—when I realize how empty the bed is, and how much I miss having her body pressed against mine. So, yeah. I guess I don't have *everything* I need.

My phone buzzes, and I set my spatula aside to retrieve my phone from my pocket. A quick glance shows that the text is from my mother asking how the ceremony went. I type a quick response and return the phone to my pocket. While my relationship with my parents is far from repaired, at least we're talking. My sister even arranged for us to have a family dinner at her place the week I return home. Four months ago, it would have taken a gun to my head to get me in the same room with my mother, father, and sister. And here I am agreeing to do it on my own free will.

I have Emily to thank for that.

Emily. The girl who I spent an entire summer running from but still can't escape.

I reach for my beer and take a long swig. Before I set out on my trip, I promised Tonya I'd call Emily after the awards ceremony. Now, I can't bring myself to do it. It's been nearly six months since she walked out of my life. While the ache in my chest feels just as raw as the day she left, somehow I've learned to live with it.

Six months is a long time. Emily, I'm sure, has moved on. If not with that guy from the bar, then with someone else. That's not something I want to know. Today is, after all, a day of letting go. Maybe Chad isn't the only one I have to stop holding onto.

I touch the bullet hanging from my neck. It's a small piece of crumpled metal but feels so much heavier, like a boulder tied around my neck, pulling me underwater. I think I'm finally ready to be free.

After finishing my burger, I follow the thin dirt path to the edge of the lake. Goose follows at my heels. Her usually upbeat demeanor is sullen, as if she knows the importance of what I have to do.

When I arrive, the sun is beginning to descend, setting the water aglow. Several boats dot the horizon. I walk to the edge of the muddy band, stopping when the toes of my boots touch the edge of the water.

I turn, half expecting to see the ghost of Chad scowling

at me, angry at what I'm about to do. But he's absent, just as he's been since the moment his mother took me into her arms.

"Chad…" My voice breaks. I feel a little stupid. At the same time, I know this is something I have to do. "I'm not going to lie and tell you I've always been grateful you saved my life. I wish it was me. I think I always will."

A crane swoops down and lands in the water several yards away. It watches me curiously.

"Anyway, I can't keep carrying you around with me. It's not fair to you or me. You wanted me to live." My throat tightens, making the words more difficult. Still, I continue. "You wanted me to live. The only way I can find to honor your choice, your *sacrifice*, is to stop holding onto you and let you go."

I unclasp the chain from my neck and hold the bullet in my fist. "We come in the dark," I mutter, reciting one of the Night Stalker mottos. "And now, I'm letting you leave in the dark."

With Goose by my side, I watch the sun sink below the horizon. The glow fades from orange to navy and then to black. In that darkness, I throw the bullet into the lake with all my might.

The heron makes a squawk of protest before taking flight.

I don't see where it falls. I hear only a distant plop of the bullet hitting the water.

Goose whines.

"He's gone," I say, reaching down to stroke the dog's head. And it's the truth. I can feel it all the way down to the marrow of my bones. Manifestation of my guilt, ghost, demon — whatever it was that followed me out of the desert, it's gone.

And that terrifies me. For the last several years, I've lived my life a haunted man. Now that I'm free, I have no idea what I'm supposed to do.

Chapter Thirty-Three

I glance at the digital clock on the Minnie Winnie's radio and mutter a curse. I hate being late. Spending an entire summer driving across the country and fishing, I got a little too comfortable with not having a schedule.

Goose sits in the passenger seat beside me, her tongue dangling out of her mouth. She squints through the rush of wind streaming through her window. After these last months we spent outdoors, I wonder how she's going to like being stuck inside a classroom.

I know I'm not looking forward to it.

A highway sign ahead alerts me Springfield is only thirty miles away.

An invisible band squeezes my chest. Returning to work isn't the only thing I'm dreading. The closer I get to home, the closer I am to *her,* the more pressure builds inside my chest.

I turn on the radio and crank the volume. With each passing mile, I grow twitchier. I need a distraction. Especially since my previous distraction—a cross-country road trip—is over.

The loud music doesn't help alleviate my anxiety. In fact, I feel even more on edge, so I turn it off. Swallowing hard, I grip the steering wheel. This wasn't supposed to happen. I was supposed to use these months to find myself and get over *her*.

Now that I'm back, I see that was never really an option. Turns out, I was only running from my unresolved feelings for her. Running but never actually escaping. Maybe I should have called her like Tonya wanted me to. But I just can't imagine Emily would want anything to do with me, not after what I did to her.

My phone rings, startling me from my thoughts. I hit the Bluetooth button on the custom stereo I had installed, and Tonya's voice fills the cab.

"Reece, where are you?"

I sigh. "There was some unexpected traffic in Nashville this morning. I should be there in about twenty-five minutes."

She tsks. "You know how Sherry is about her faculty meetings. She's going to be pissed you're late."

"I know."

"You should have come home sooner."

I know that, too. Despite planning to get over Emily while I was gone that summer, part of me was worried my feelings for her would come rushing back the moment I returned. I had wanted to put that off for as long as I could. Too late.

"Tell you what," I say, "I'll pick up a box of donuts on the way in. That should smooth things over."

"I have a better idea," Tonya says. "There's this new bakery off of Walnut. It's two blocks away from school. They sell these bacon bun things that are to *die* for. Pick up a dozen, and I bet you Sherry won't even mention you being late."

Inwardly I grimace. Driving down Walnut will force me to drive past the coffee shop where Emily works. Surely,

Tonya knows that. I open my mouth to tell her I'd rather face Sherry's wrath for being late, but she beats me to it.

"Grab the buns, and I'll see you when you get here." She hangs up before I can argue.

I mutter another curse. She's cunning, that Tonya.

Goose cocks her head, her tail thumping against the seat.

"Looks like we have a pit stop to make," I tell her.

Twenty minutes later, I see Emily's coffee shop up ahead. I tighten my jaw, clenching the muscles as I keep my eyes focused on the road. If thinking about her is this hard, I can't imagine what it would do to me to see her through the window.

Unconsciously, I slow the RV down as I drive past. I force my foot back on the accelerator while what feels like every cell in my body strains for me to stop the vehicle. I make it past the shop, and the knot inside my gut loosens, letting me breathe easier. I mentally congratulate myself for winning this round. Unfortunately, I have this internal battle to look forward to every day of the upcoming school year.

With the coffee shop well behind me, I search for a bakery among the various shopping malls and restaurants I pass. It doesn't take long before I spot a sign perched along the side of the road reading Senelė Bakery.

Strange name for a bakery, I think as I pull the Minnie Winnie into the nearly full lot. Only a couple spots are available, none of them wide enough for me, and I'm forced to park off in the grass.

The blue two-story house, now converted to a bakery, has a wrap-around porch, complete with a porch swing and bird feeders. Several people sit at tables outside, sipping coffee, reading, and scrolling through their phones. The smell of bread wafts from the door and is enough to make my mouth water before Goose and I even set foot on the porch.

I glance through the large window in the door and

mentally groan. The waiting area is packed with people bunched around the glass cases of baked goods. My pulse skips several beats, and I consider abandoning my mission.

Goose nudges my hand, urging me on.

She's right. I made it this far, might as well keep going.

I open the door and step inside.

If I thought it smelled good outside, it's nothing compared to the scent of honey, bread, pretzels, and coffee inside. One whiff and I realize this isn't the average bakery. There's not a single cupcake, brownie, or donut in sight. There are, however, bacon buns, pretzels, honey cakes, and various other pastries labeled with names I can't pronounce.

I grab a paper number from the dispenser. While the waiting area is packed, the line moves quickly. Soon enough, my number is called.

The girl behind the counter is young, barely out of high school. She reminds me a bit of Emily with her tattoos and piercings. But Em's hair is short, curly, and blond, while this girl's dark braid hangs nearly to her waist.

"I need a dozen bacon buns." I quickly scan the display case. Since I'm here, might as well make it worth my while. "And a dozen pretzels."

Nodding, she grabs a piece of cardboard and folds it into a box. With gloved hands, she starts placing bacon buns into the box only to come up short. "Hang on," she tells me. Glancing over her shoulder at a pair of swinging doors, she shouts, "We need more bacon buns!"

"Just a sec," a voice calls back.

My chest tightens. Too much gunfire in the desert screwed up my ears. I must be mistaken.

The doors swing wide and Emily walks out. Her hair is tied back with a green bandana, and flour is streaked across her cheeks. She holds a large baking sheet with several buns balanced on top. "These are straight from the oven, so they're still hot."

The dark-haired girl nods and begins removing the buns with a set of tongs.

My first instinct is to run, but I find I can't convince my feet to move. So far, she hasn't seen me. But that ends the second Goose whines.

Emily glances at my dog. She studies her with interest before her eyes track the length of her leash, to my hand, then travel up my body until they come to rest on my face. Her lips part and the edge of her baking sheet dips toward the floor as several buns topple off the side.

"Emily! What the hell?" The dark-haired girl grabs a nearby towel and yanks the baking sheet away from Emily before she loses any more buns.

"I, uh…fuck," Emily says, her eyes never leaving mine.

I wonder if Tonya knew Emily worked here before sending me on this fool's errand.

"Em, I'm so sorry." It's true, I realize. I'm sorry for showing up and surprising her like I did, but the moment the words leave my mouth, it dawns on me I'm sorry for so much more than that. "I'm just…God, I'm so sorry. I'm just so sorry."

The customers gathered in the lobby fall silent. Many look away.

Emily's face crumples, and she puts a hand to her mouth. "You have a dog," she says, her voice cracking.

"You have a bakery," I reply.

She laughs. "Yeah."

I spent an entire summer running from her. All that time, it never occurred to me, when I finally saw her, it would feel like I never left. "I missed you." After lying to myself for so long, I'm surprised at how easily the truth finally comes out.

She drops her hands and takes a tentative step toward the counter dividing us. "I missed you, too."

"I made a mistake."

"Me, too."

"I never should have…"

"I know." She cuts me off.

For the first time since the desert, the people surrounding us fade away. There's only me and her. And such precious, little time. I refuse to waste anymore.

"I had to get away," I tell her. "I had to figure some stuff out."

She hops onto the counter and swings her feet over the edge. "Me, too. What did you figure out?"

"I want to stop pissing my life away. I want a life, a *real* one. What did you figure out?"

She laughs. "Exactly the same thing."

I step toward her. "You have any space in your new, real, life for me?"

Grinning, she says, "I might be able to make some room."

I can't stand it. I cannot physically tolerate the space dividing us anymore. Before she can react, I drop Goose's leash and snatch her off the counter. My knee twinges, but I ignore the pain. Because it's worth it.

Every last drop of pain.

Worth it.

Chapter Thirty-Four

I imagined all the things I'd do when I saw Reece again—
pretend not to know him, blow him off, flip him the bird, key
his bike, and more. Never, in every fantasy played out in my
head, did I imagine myself allowing him to pick me up off my
feet, let alone kiss me.

Then again, I never knew I wanted to own my own bakery.
I guess part of growing up is not only discovering yourself, but
also discovering what it is you want.

And I want Reece.

I'm vaguely aware of my employee's shocked gasp and
the stares of our patrons as I curl my fingers into Reece's hair
and his lips meet mine. Maybe I look unprofessional, but I'm
past the point of caring.

I touch the stubble on his usually smooth cheeks. His hair
is longer, the ends just curling around the bottom of his ears.
And his skin is darker, too. One thing hasn't changed, though.
His kiss is just as searing as I remember, and I find myself

melting into it.

"I was an idiot," Reece murmurs against my neck when we finally part lips. "I was trying to push you away."

"I think I was looking for a reason to be pushed."

He nods, setting me back on the ground. "So how about it then, will you marry me?"

"Cute," I tell him, elbowing him in the ribs. "You're a jokester now. Who are you, and what have you done with Reece?"

He grins. "I was funny once. Feels like a lifetime ago. I guess you're going to have to get to know me all over again."

"I've been sober for three months." I throw my hands wide. "It turns out I do have ambition. I'm kind of obsessed with this place. I think you're going to have to get to know me, too."

"Fair enough."

"If we do this again," I say, wrapping my arms around his neck, "I want to do things differently."

He arches an eyebrow. "Yeah?"

"This time I want strings," I say, leaning in for another kiss. "Lots and lots of strings.

"You got it," he replies with a grin. "I'll entangle you in so many strings you'll never get away from me again."

Epilogue

Six months later

I'm lounging on the small bed, reading a book in the tiny camper, when the door bursts open. Goose bounds inside, followed by Reece and an armful of fish.

I squeal as an icy gust fills the small room. "Close the door," I cry, scrambling to wrap myself in a blanket.

He grins. "I come bearing gifts." He holds his fish out like a trophy.

I wrinkle my noise. "Your gift stinks. Literally."

He laughs. "I'll put them out in the cooler." He disappears out the door and returns a moment later fish-free. He plops down on the pull-out bench and begins removing his boots. "Did you miss me?"

I grin. "Always."

He returns my smile. "You could have come out on the lake with me."

I pull the blanket tighter. "One fishing trip a decade is enough for me, thank you very much."

He makes a face. "And yet you're making me go to a baking tradeshow tomorrow? How is that fair?"

"Really? Let's think about that. Icy temperatures, bugs, and smelly fish versus indoor heating, working plumbing, and delicious food. There's no contest."

"Speaking of delicious food... We have any of that *kugelis* stuff left?"

"In the mini fridge."

He makes a beeline for the fridge, pulls out the red Tupperware container, opens the lid, smells the *kugelis*, and smiles. "What is it about this that makes it so magical?"

"That would be my grandma's secret ingredient—bacon fat."

"I think I love your grandma."

I laugh. "Me, too."

His face grows serious, and he sets the *kugelis* aside. "Em, I love you, too."

My breath stills in my chest, and I'm sure I've misheard him. "What?"

Without using his cane, he takes slow steps toward me before climbing next to me on the bed. "I do. I have. For a long time. I guess I've been afraid to say anything for fear of scaring you off again. But I think you should know. I love you, Emily Garrett."

"I love you, too." And I do. I've known practically from the first date. But as someone so terrified of commitment, I was too afraid to tell him. Maybe even more afraid to tell myself.

"Listen"—he takes my hands—"I know you don't want a guy who's going to control you. And I would never be that guy, Em. I love your surprises—the way you keep me guessing what you're going to do next. This is your journey. I just want to go on the trip with you."

He motions to Goose. With her tail wagging, the black

Labrador trots over. I notice she's carrying something in her mouth, but I can't tell what it is until the she deposits it onto my lap. A box. A tiny black box. The kind rings come in.

I gasp. "What the hell is that?"

"I wish I could get down on a knee," Reece says. "Given my bum knee, I wouldn't be able to get back up again." He opens the box, revealing a raw-cut stone flashing every color of the rainbow. "It's a moonstone," he says, answering my unasked question. "A unique stone for my unique girl. I know you have a thing about commitment, but, Emily, I know there's no other woman for me. This just feels right."

He takes the thin gold band out of the box and holds the ring out to me. "Emily Garrett, will you let me ride shotgun?"

"Yes." The word leaves my tongue before I have a chance to think about it. He wasn't kidding when he said it felt right—more than right, actually. Perfect. Reece is the man who will stand beside me, never in front of me, blocking the way. Just like I'm prepared to stand beside him, to support him when he needs to lean on me.

He slides the ring down my ring finger. It's too big, so I slip it onto my middle finger instead.

"I guess we'll have to get it sized," Reece says.

"Nope. I think it looks better there."

He laughs. "Whatever you want."

That gives me pause. It's funny to think how far I've come in the last year. From a girl who wanted no attachments and had no idea what to do with her life, to finally figuring things out. "This."

He quirks an eyebrow. "What?"

"This." I hold my arms out wide. "The stinky fish, the RV, the bakery, you, the dog, this life." I wrap my arms around his neck and draw him to me for what I hope will be one of a million kisses. "This, and whatever is left to come. That's what I want."

Acknowledgments

As always, I have to thank my incredible husband for his bottomless well of patience and support. You taught me that true love exists outside the covers of romance novels.

I want to thank my amazing agent, Nicole Resciniti, for her support, encouragement, and for the two a.m. hotel lobby conversations over a glass of crown.

This book wouldn't have been possible without the genius insight of editor extraordinaire Liz Pelletier. I can't thank you enough for making me a part of the Entangled family.

Lydia Sharp, thank you for the comma addiction intervention. I need a twelve-step program.

Heather Riccio, thank you for always having my back. And Rhianna Walker, thank you so much for that cup of coffee. You made me feel like a rock star.

As always, this book is only partially mine. The rest belongs to my amazing critique partners, Brad Cook, T.W. Fendley, and Jennifer Lynn. Your brilliant insights made this book what it is.

About the Author

At seventeen Cole found herself homeless with only a beat-up Volkswagen Jetta and a bag of Goodwill clothing to her name. The only things that got her through the nights she spent parked in truck stops and cornfields were the stacks of books she checked out from the library along with her trusty flashlight. Because of the reprieve these books gave her from her troubles, Cole vowed to become a writer so she could provide the same escape to readers who needed a break the reality of their own lives.

www.colegibsen.com

Discover more New Adult titles from Entangled Embrace...

AVENGED
a novel by Marnee Blake

Special-ops soldier Nick Degrassi blames himself for Kitty Laughton's capture, and he'll do whatever he can to free the quiet beauty, but close quarters and a shared secret bring an attraction that neither of them expected. With the organization that started it all making mercenaries for hire, Nick and Kitty must save themselves and stop a madman...before it's too late.

LAST WISH
a novel by Erin Butler

Nothing feels right. Not since my best friend died and I fucked up the one promise asked me to make. Now my life is so fucking empty. Then *she* walks into the bar, all bright beauty and sweet lips made for kissing. Em Stewart is a complication...one I need to avoid. No matter how hard I try, I can't resist her, and our unexpected road trip sure as hell isn't helping my cause. But I'll be damned if I screw up my first chance at something real...

THIS BOOK WILL CHANGE YOUR LIFE
a novel by Amanda Weaver

College is where Hannah Gregory plans to follow in her dad's footsteps as a chemistry prodigy—except she bombs her first test. And now her future isn't so certain. Salvation comes from an unlikely place—a used bookstore and the sexy college senior who works there. Ben Fisher is trapped in a life mapped out for him. Then he meets the beautiful Hannah. And for the first time, he knows what it means to truly want something. But freedom comes with a cost, and it isn't long before their carefully planned lives begin to fall apart...

Wanting More

a *Love on Campus* novel by Jessica Ruddick

Bri Welch likes to play it safe. I don't. She's wound tight, and I'm all about a good party. But there's something about her that makes me want to pull those uptight layers away one-by-delicious-one. But the worst thing is she makes me want more…

Also by Cole Gibsen...

WRITTEN ON MY HEART

LIFE UNAWARE

62345427R00139

Made in the USA
Lexington, KY
05 April 2017